LAST CALL
IN THE CITY OF BRIDGES

A NOVEL

SALVATORE PANE

BRADDOCK
AVENUE
BOOKS

UNCOMMON BOOKS · UNCOMMON READERS

The characters and events in this book are fictitious. Any similarity to real persons, living or dead, is coincidental and not intended by the author.

Printed in the United States of America
10 9 8 7 6 5 4 3 2 1

FIRST EDITION, November 2012

ISBN-10: 0615679323
ISBN-13: 978-0-615-67932-7

Sections of this book have appeared in slightly different forms in the following publication:

"This is How the Century is Born," *Annalemma* (7).

Braddock Avenue Books
PO Box 502
Braddock, PA 15204

Book design by Joel W. Coggins
Webcomics by Lamair Nash

www.braddockavenuebooks.com

LAST CALL IN THE CITY OF BRIDGES

"We even find it difficult to be human beings, men with real flesh and blood of *our* own; we are ashamed of it, we think it a disgrace, and are always striving to be some unprecedented kind of generalized human being. We are born dead."

—FYODOR DOSTOEVSKY, *Notes From Underground*

"Excuse me? Was you saying something? Nu uh! Can't tell me nothing. Nu uh! Can't tell me nothing."

—KANYE WEST, "Can't Tell Me Nothing"

Election Night:
The Prologue

It was supposed to be the greatest night of our lives. By our, I mean my entire generation, all those unlucky souls raised on the 8-bit wastelands manufactured by Nintendo, all those boys and girls who watched the Berlin Wall crumble in kindergarten, the Twin Towers in high school. Overeducated, Twittering, viral. We were in the process of becoming beams of light. Too fast. Too quick for the longwinded ruminations of cinema, the sluggish pace of weekly television installments, the painful seconds it took to scan blog entries of celebrities and friends alike. We were a generation of microbloggers. 140 character rants. Election Night was supposed to be our moment, but not all of us were ready to believe. Not people like me, scorned lovers who lost their voting virginity to the 2004 presidential election. By the eve of the Obama age, that loss still burned bright. But we longed to call ourselves whole again, something more than receptacles for networks and terabytes.

I lived in Squirrel Hill on the east end of Pittsburgh. A place with cobblestone streets and Orthodox families, ancient synagogues where Rabbis still cared about the proclamations of an absent God. My old roommate Oz was long gone, but I still clung desperately to his possessions, the apartment transforming more and more into a mausoleum with each new day.

While election results scrolled across the TV screen, I went to the bookshelf where I kept the booze. I liked to run my finger down the spines of Oz's books and think important thoughts while fixing myself a drink. *Understanding Media: The Extensions of Man. Cybernetics: or Control and Communication in the Animal and the Machine. Gramophone, Film, Typewriter.* By the time I returned to the couch, Obama had already won. I held up my highball in toast. I'd seen Humphrey Bogart order one in a black and white film and had started drinking them while reading articles on the internet that foretold the end of the world: the Large Hadron Collider, food riots, Al Gore and the magic of global warming, nuclear holocaust, the sixth extinction, the collapse of the oil industry, etc. etc.

I knew Obama's victory would be a moment I'd always remember, and to celebrate, I thumped my knee and clapped softly three times. I logged onto Twitter and typed *WOOOOOO* but was drowned out by the collective noise of a million techno liberals orgasming simultaneously. Someone in my feed tweeted about heading to the Squirrel Cage for victory drinks.

The Squirrel Cage?

The Squirrel Cage!

It had been months since I'd ventured inside that lovable bar just seven blocks away from my home, since I'd experienced firsthand the smoke, rust and charm of a bar that was hip but not too hip. There's nothing about the Cage that makes it inherently unique. There are a dozen places like it in Pittsburgh, a thousand in other American metropolises, a million in the small towns lurking amongst the shadows between Los Angeles and New York City. But the Cage possessed a sour *je ne se quoi* because my friends and I had grown up there and discovered things about each other we never wanted to know, secrets that prevented us from ever being civil again.

OBAMA!

I felt him calling to me from beyond the edge of my staticy television screen, his body shaded translucent blue like Obi-Wan Kenobi. *Go to the Squirrel Cage, Michael. Do it for me, the B-Man. Do it for my daughters. They're cute, right? Super cute. And may the force be with you.* If I left immediately, I could catch his acceptance speech at the Cage, I could bear witness to something magical with a room of drunken, joyous peers. I buttoned my pea coat and went out, the cold shocking me sober. Cars honked as they sped by. People stood on porches and banged pots and pans. Students poured out of the makeshift Democratic Headquarters amid dozens of red, white and blue balloons.

The Squirrel Cage was packed with twenty-somethings cool enough to name check obscure bands with low run EPs, to wear vintage threads from the thrift shop next door, to recognize that all emotion had turned irrelevant in the rising tide of millennial irony. We valued apathy. Caring about things was beyond the point, the zombie ramblings of generations past. But in this moment everyone understood that it was acceptable to relent, that on this day we would not be judged. We hooted and hollered. We stomped our feet. Someone played "Rock Lobster" on the electronic jukebox. I shoved past the crowd and ordered another highball.

In walked Ivy Chase, a gust of cold air trailing her. She saw me at the bar and stopped midstride. I blinked at her.

Once, twice, three times. What did exes ever have to say to one another? The sweet roundness of Ivy's body was hidden by a sweater, overcoat, and three plaid scarves. She rubbed her elbow and looked behind her. I knew she was considering leaving on my account, and because I couldn't deal with that humiliation I raised my glass and waved, a splash of whiskey wetting the lapel of my coat. Behind me on the television, John McCain was conceding the presidency to boos and screams in Phoenix, Arizona: the nuclear desert of the McCarthy era.

Now it was Ivy's turn to blink. Her hair was different. Shorter. It framed her face. She'd always had gorgeous hair—blonde: soft and fluffy when straightened, thick curls otherwise—and I'm not ashamed to admit I was suddenly filled with longing, the old sensations that had blinded us for so long. For the first time in months, my old flame Ivy Chase smiled at me, her girl-next-door grin full of dimples and big teeth. I'd always had a thing for girls with big teeth. Ivy Chase. I should have known!

She came over and rocked back and forth on her kicks. "Crazy isn't it?"

"I haven't been here in months."

She narrowed her eyes. "I meant the election."

"Obama?"

"Obama."

A boy in a ratty sports coat squeezed between us, a bottle of beer raised high above his head like a promise. Ivy placed her hand on her hip and smiled again. Her eyes were blue and I kept trying to look past her, to see someone I recognized roaming around the Cage, one of the many graveyards of my fast evaporating youth.

"You want to catch up?" she asked.

I shrugged. She was twenty-two—three years my junior—but still had a way of making me feel like a child. "I'll buy you a beer," I offered.

"No thanks."

She called the bartender over. From the way he playfully slapped his cheek at the sight of her, I knew she hadn't been here recently either. I was good with details, which was something Ivy had liked about me once. We headed toward the back and stood between two pinball machines, huddled so that no one would jostle us on their way past. Arcade buzzers and beeps served as the soundtrack, the electronic dissonance of our flat-lined love.

"Have you seen any of the old gang or is everyone still crazy off the grid?" she asked.

"I haven't seen anyone in months."

She sipped through the foam of her lager and bopped her head as some hipster played every song off *Born to Run*. I held my glass over the wet spot on my jacket and hoped Ivy didn't notice. Her golden cross glittered under the pale light of the bar and shone against her porcelain skin. She turned to the front and gave a great big wave. I bargained with whatever higher power might listen to me for Ivy not to be meeting some guy here, that I wouldn't be forced to have my nose rubbed in her uncontrollable happiness. But no, it was worse. It was Elaine Tedesco.

"You," she said.

"What up?"

She poked me in the chest. "You are absolutely disgusting, Michael. My mother told me what you said to her and I don't buy a word of it. And that *thing* you made on the internet! What's wrong with you? Are you even human?"

"But but but but but but but-"

"Just stop." She put her back to me and touched Ivy's forearm. "I'll meet up with you when you're done with this..." She paused here to find the perfect word, but it never came. She shook her head, turned on her heels and left.

"Guess she hasn't gotten over it," Ivy said.

"You know about all that? With her mother?"

"Of course. We had a long talk about all things Michael Bishop related."

"You were the one who told me to go see her."

"I told you to be honest."

To Ivy's credit, she didn't look disgusted by me, only a little saddened, maybe even interested, the way people slow down alongside a car crash to gawk at the unthinkable damage. And I suddenly wanted to apologize for everything that had happened. Not just between the two of us, or even our broken circle of friends, but between everyone in the entirety of human existence.

"I'm so, *so* sorry."

"I know, Michael."

The jukebox cut out and everyone hushed. There he was. President-Elect Barack Hussein Obama, a sea of Chicago awed before him. He opened his golden mouth and made everything beautiful again. *If there is anyone out there who still doubts that America is a place where all things are possible, who still wonders if the dream of our founders is alive in our time, who still questions the power of our democracy, tonight is your answer.* He gave us something to believe in, the tiny shuddering hope that we—the hip, the young, the beautiful and free—could climb out of our media caves and once again see the light we had come to know so intimately in childhood. I watched people clap, watched Ivy turn to the wondrous rays of the almighty television, close enough to smell her perfume, an item she once compulsively hid from me. She used to tell me it was mystery that kept relationships alive. I wondered if she still believed that and tried to envision a parallel universe where we'd stayed together. Would we have made it? Would we have been happy? Obama spoke. He spoke some more. We listened. *This is our chance to answer that call. This is our moment.* I touched the small of Ivy's back. That inward swoop was my favorite part of her body, an intimate place only I saw exposed, but innocent enough to

8

stroke in public. She didn't respond. But it was the least and most I could do, a bittersweet moment, something we could fondly remember after an unhappy ending. And when the speech was over, the whole bar remained silent, listening to the commentators discuss the legion of problems the Obama Administration would have to face: the escalating financial crisis, dual wars abroad, the potential death of the planet. Can he do it, the news anchor asked, can he pull us out of this mess? The analyst shook his head, said he wasn't sure, told us to enjoy tonight because there were dark times ahead.

How I Celebrated My
Twenty-Fifth Birthday

Ten months before the election, I packed my laptop into my messenger bag and headed into the cobblestone of Squirrel Hill to celebrate my birthday. It was a Saturday in January, which meant layers, layers, layers. And even though there were two coffeehouses a block away from my house—a Starbucks even nerds avoided because of its corporate heritage, and the 61C Café with all those white-sneakered undergrads rehashing Deleuze—I made the seven block journey to Arefa's on account of the barista: the always lovely, sometimes feisty Sloan Smith. Also, I went there to be seen, to let others know that I had terribly vital work to complete even on the weekend, even on my birthday. Sloan smiled at me from behind the counter, but I didn't return it. I was too focused on the disappointment: Arefa's was empty. I plugged my laptop into the wall and ordered a latte.

"That'll be three eighty-four," Sloan said.

"Really, S? On my birthday?"

"Yes, friend. Even on your birthday."

I pouted and handed her a crumpled five. Sloan Smith possessed the most beautiful face I had ever seen. Olive skin with full lips, blue eyes, round cheeks, a product of a Jewish father and Italian mother. Her dark hair fell in clusters above her shoulders, and her glasses were just retro enough to make her look intelligent without seeming pretentious. We'd met as freshmen at the University of Pittsburgh in Tower A, twelfth floor. She was the first native Pittsburgher I ever met. Her build was somewhat stocky, a flaw that lifted her above all the pretty girls with their sorority shirts and Ugg boots.

"I forgot to tell you." Her voice was deep and scratchy. She no longer smoked but sounded like she'd gone through ten packs a day since Watergate. "One of my best friends from high school moved back to Pittsburgh. I've known her since grade school."

"You had friends growing up?"

She didn't bother with a comeback. Every friend I've ever had has at some point learned to ignore my sarcasm or move on.

"She went to Fordham," Sloan explained. "In New York City. But we kept in touch on Facebook. She's three years behind us but graduated a semester early. I was thinking maybe she could tag along tonight for your birthday. Meet the gang and all that? She's cool. I vouch."

I took a seat and flexed open my laptop. "On a scale of one to ten where ten is me and one is Hitler, where does this young lady friend of yours fall?"

"Eight. She's really bubbly, very smart. Total babe. Ivy Chase."

I nodded and checked my e-mail. There was an electronic greeting card from my parents. A flash animation of a turtle danced across the screen and told me to have a radical birthday. I typed a reminder in gmail to send my parents a thank you note. "Are you trying to set me up, S?"

"No. Don't even make an attempt. She's got a boyfriend back in New York."

"Boyfriend's just a word."

She rolled her eyes at me, although I wasn't quite sure why. Sloan had a peculiar habit of introducing me to women and then undercutting my chances, writing the young lady in question off as involved, insane, manipulative, or any number of turn offs. Usually, she did this in front of Noah Black, her boyfriend, and I wondered if it was because of that one night so long ago, the night we never spoke of, the drunken evening when our platonic friendship slipped into something else entirely. Sloan Smith. My most important relationship with a woman who was not my mother.

"I think," she said, "you should stop worrying about women and spend some time working on yourself."

"I haven't dated anyone in two years."

"And the female population of Pittsburgh thanks you." She came out from behind the counter and sat across from me. "You know I love you, right? And I don't mean this to criticize, but I don't think you're ready for a relationship right now."

"You really know how to celebrate a guy's birthday."

"I'm serious. You have so many shields up all the time. You deflect everything. You're Teflon. I know there's this really great person inside of you, but you never let him through past all the jokes and sarcasm."

"Oh, so is Noah completely open and above all my jokes and sarcasm and deflection?"

She returned behind her counter. "Noah is Noah, and we all love him. By the way, I don't know if you've checked my feed lately, but I'm up to 8,000 subscribers."

She was referring to the infamous video project that had taken over her otherwise mundane existence. "Twenty-

Something Barista Counts to 250,000," a video stream where Sloan sat in front of her webcam and counted. Whenever she had free time, she picked up where she left off. At last count she'd hit 177,489.

"Wow," I said. "That's probably the most exciting thing I've ever heard in my entire life!"

"See," she said with a big smile. "That's what I'm talking about. Deflection."

"You're the one counting on the internet, S."

Before she could defend her project, I plugged my ear buds into my laptop and streamed a concept album about robots in a post-human landscape. I'd grown up an only child and had never gotten used to the relentless chattering of other human beings.

On Facebook, I found a link Oz had posted to my wall. This is how we communicated. Not just Oz and me, but every single person I knew. We traded links, read each other's blogs, followed Twitter feeds, bookmarked Lifecast streams. There was no need for actual conversation even though everyone had so much to say. Oz's link showed an inviting picture of Mr. Rogers and I clicked it with low anxiety and a cautious hope.

DID MR. ROGERS RUIN AN ENTIRE GENERATION?

By Patty Kanyuck

Won't you be my neighbor? Not if I can help it. Researchers at the University of Utah's psychology department have completed a study suggesting that telling young children they're special may do more harm than good. The researchers hypothesize that this fundamental problem goes beyond the classroom and has roots in a late '70s media shift, of which *Mr. Rogers' Neighborhood* was at the forefront, where children's programs began to focus more on individuality in-stead of responsibilities and good behavior.

UU researchers studied four thousand young men and women between the ages of 18 and 25, posing questions such as, "Do you consider yourself more special than others?", "Do you deserve more happiness than your peers?" and "Who has more inherent worth: an American or a foreigner?"

Dr. Albert Tompkins, principal investigator of the study, discovered that a whopping 79% of participants were more likely to respond positively to questions reaffirming their inherent uniqueness, yet these participants were also found to be less happy with their jobs and partners and more likely to be depressed or contemplating suicide.

"The results are alarming," Dr. Tompkins reported. "We asked the same questions a research team posed to similar demographics back in 1965, and the percentage of young people who believe that destiny has something special in store for them has quadrupled.

"Telling children that everyone's special may seem like a smart idea on paper," Dr. Tompkins said. "But as we've seen, it leads to feelings of inadequacy and even mental breakdowns when the child fails to meet expectations of achievement. We need to rethink how we positively reinforce children immediately."

But is there any hope for the current generation? Dr. Tompkins fears that the current culture will result in a lifetime of diminished expectations for this age cohort. Apparently, Mr. Rogers was wrong. There are a ton of people in the world just like you, and they're not fine just the way they are.

Thanks...? I typed on Oz's wall. Why would anyone send that to somebody on their birthday? Maybe it was a joke, but I didn't take much stock in the article either way. It was published by the *Utah Observer*, not *Slate*. I clicked out of Firefox.

Customers had begun drifting inside the coffee shop. Two guys in cardigans and then three Asian girls with Kanye West glasses, the kind with plastic slits and no prescriptions. This was why I'd gone to Arefa's instead of staying at home and brewing Folgers—to see and be seen—and it was time to get to work. I loaded Photoshop 7 and selected my web comic template. For an entire year, I'd written and drawn a weekly comic strip: http://MichaelBishopsWackyWorldOf RobotHumanHybrids.wordpress.org

It chronicled the lives of three "hipster robots" and I

averaged 200 unique visitors a day. I didn't focus on that anemic number or how those hits most likely represented friends stumbling in through links I posted on Facebook. Instead, I thought about how noble it was that I trudged on with a creative endeavor while subtitling DVDs Monday through Friday, a 9-5 that sucked my spirit dry day after agonizing day!

But no one noticed me and finally, regretfully, there was nothing to do but the unglamorous work of creating a web comic, the tedious lines and shading, the precise word balloons, the quirky pacing and offbeat characterization I deserved to be known for. It took an hour and a half to finish up, but when it was done, I'd concocted the single greatest achievement in the history of mankind.

I finished my second latte and kept the web comic on my browser hoping someone would walk by and notice it. An hour passed. A petite girl in fishnets asked if she could borrow the salt. I sulked home and crawled under my covers until it was time to go out for my birthday. I couldn't fall asleep. I just lay there, hoping against hope that I was more than meets the eye. Like Pinocchio, I desperately wanted to become human.

My roommate Oz and I walked under the streetlights en route to the Cage. He was a touch heavy, thick in the hips and chest. He had messy curly hair, a beard peppered with premature grays, and was working toward a PhD at Pitt where he studied digital media theory and something called ludic pedagogy. I didn't understand much of what he was learning. What little I could decipher centered on how mankind had not truly been human for centuries, how first person narratives were the first inventions that took people outside of themselves and into virtual worlds. Even glasses were a way of seeing through inorganic, mechanical eyes. What was abundantly clear was that spending every waking hour in a cubicle in the Cathedral of Learning with oily grad students had turned Owen Osborne III sullen and disagreeable.

"I read the article you posted on my wall," I said.

"What did you think?"

"I don't know. A little depressing. Makes sense though. You think of our parents? Our grandparents? They didn't seem to care about doing something important or being unique. All they wanted was a family and a house."

"See, that's where I think the article's wrong. I don't think we're really any different, there's just more time now for people to screw around between getting a degree and starting a family. There's this ten year period that didn't really exist before. The Odyssey Period some people are calling it."

"So you think we should all just get married straight out of college?"

Oz lit a Lucky Strike. "Not totally sure yet. I'm working all these issues out on Twitter if you want to follow along."

I tried to look contemplative. Oz and I were going into our seventh year of being roommates, ever since I traded Scranton for Pittsburgh when we'd both been assigned to

Room 1212 in Tower A. We met Sloan the very first weekend and struck up a friendship. Oz majored in English and I minored in it, so I possessed a certain level of tolerance for these types of pretentious conversations. But sometimes he spoke about our generation as if it were some cultural artifact he could deconstruct and diagnose. And lately, he'd taken to sleep walking. He'd get up in the middle of the night and roam around the house, rearranging our furniture.

Oz cupped his hand around his snakeskin lighter, his fingers trembling.

Even on a Saturday night, the second floor of the Cage was empty. There were bigger tables up there and the music wasn't quite so loud, a safeguard against some hipster playing the entirety of Styx's *Kilroy Was Here* as we'd done in the past, snickering at people who groaned at the opening chords of each new song. I was turning twenty-five! The time for snickers—the laughter and the candy—had come to a bitter end.

Sloan and her boyfriend Noah Black showed up at the same time as the first pitcher of Yuengling. As Sloan greeted us with complaints about the coffee shop and lack of decent jobs for art history majors, I leaned in close to Noah and gave him a nice, manly shake. Noah was twenty-eight, had gone to college in Jersey on a DII basketball scholarship. He was also a native Pittsburgher who had been introduced to Sloan at a church picnic after our sophomore year of college. He did something involving computers at my office and had landed me the gig in the first place. Noah Black, the older brother I'd always wanted, the Wolverine to my Spider-Man. He wished me a happy birthday and nodded toward Sloan still yammering on to Oz.

"You want to do birthday shots?" Noah asked.

Downstairs, he ordered us Three Wise Men—a combination of the named whiskies: Johnnie Walker, Jim Beam and Jack Daniels. We slugged them back and set our empties upside down on the bar. One of the reasons Noah and I got along so well was our mutual love of drinking our balls off. Oz and Sloan possessed limits. They'd long outgrown boozing beyond a certain precipice, beyond waking up hunched over the toilet and dry heaving all morning. Noah and I had not, and when the two of us went out after work in the Southside, we usually ended up stumbling back home or worse, taking rides from random girls and getting stoned in the undergraduate slums.

Sloan stuck her head over the fenced edge of the second floor and mimed shooting us with her index finger. It was no secret she didn't approve of our shenanigans. Noah ignored her and ordered a beer. "Ball and chain, right?" He nudged me in the elbow. "See that girl who just came in? The blonde? Cute, huh? That's Sloan's friend from grade school. That's Ivy Chase."

And then…

I am not the type of man drawn in by what traditionalists classify as beauty. I'm rarely attracted to supermodels or pop stars, and maybe that's because I have no chance with them. But I'd like to believe that there's something deeper there, that they don't appear particularly real to me. Deficiencies are what make people beautiful because they heighten what's inherently attractive. I've always been the guy who chases after girls with glasses. Before that: girls with braces. Occasionally girls with wonderfully round stomachs or girls with feet crooked and maimed from years of dance. I can't explain it. I'm no Freud.

But one look at Ivy Chase and it was obvious she'd found a way to lure in everyone through sheer wholesomeness alone. Blonde bangs, blue eyes, and a perennial smile. Wide hipped, and forgive me, just the tiniest bit plump in a black cardigan and red dress. Noah waved her over, so I sucked in my paunch and puffed out my chest. I put my hands at my waist and slid both thumbs into my pockets, my cool guy stance. I'd practiced it in front of the mirror dozens of times, quoting badass lines from badass movies. Schwarzenegger lines.

Noah introduced us. Ivy outstretched her slightly moist hand. "So I hear it's your birthday," she said. "How old are you? Forty-seven?"

"Nah, I'm turning nineteen." I nodded toward the bartender. "Keep it on the dl."

She didn't laugh. I coughed into my fist. Noah suggested we head upstairs and we did so in devastating silence.

Sloan and Ivy made a big production out of seeing each other again, but then we got down to the business at hand: to hear ourselves speak, to be contemporary, accounted for, understood and loved. Oz lit another Lucky Strike and we were off.

"You know what's really been bugging me?" he asked. "When I'm ninety, you'll be able to hand me a Nintendo with *Super Mario Brothers* and I'll still remember where every warp pipe's hidden. I'll remember the noise the dog makes in *Duck Hunt* when you mess up." He took a long, thoughtful gulp of his beer and raised a single finger so we wouldn't get the impression he'd come to story's end. "But I'm only twenty-five and I can barely remember what my old man's voice sounded like. Isn't that crazy? But I still remember that 8-bit dog."

It was good to see him this way, jokey, ironic, a reminder of the fun guy Oz had been in college. And often he still was that person, that good natured chum we remembered. But sometimes—especially after receiving a particularly negative comment on one of his opus-like papers—Oz would descend into a murky sadness, a reminder of my best friend from high school, Keith Tedesco, a wound I'd never told my Pittsburgh friends about.

"I've been thinking a lot about Batman recently," Noah said. "If the Wayne family was so rich, why didn't they have a car pick them up at the movies before they got shot? And why would Thomas Wayne lead his wife and young son down a street named Crime Alley?"

"It's offensive to poor people," Oz said. "The Waynes are capitalists. They created Gotham's lower class. Then they get killed and in their wake there's this trust fund baby terrorizing the proletariat with bats and the power of myth. It's George Bushian fear mongering at its finest."

"Can we not insult Batman on my birthday, please?"

"They're not always like this," Sloan said to Ivy.

Noah offered to refill her glass. She declined. "So, Ivy? What kind of cars have you owned?"

I leaned in close to Ivy. My arm brushed hers and I felt sixteen, panicky and anxious. "Noah has this theory that you can understand a person just by knowing what cars they've owned."

Using only her eyes, Ivy invited each and every one of us into her sphere of squeaky-clean influence. "Well this should be easy then. I've only owned one. '96 Geo Metro. It stalls every three out of ten times I try to drive it. What does that say?"

Noah wiggled his eyebrows. "Michael, why don't you take a stab?"

"Ok. '96 Geo Metro says you're practical. You don't care about money. It's what's on the inside that counts."

Sloan pinched her nose. "Super corny."

"He's wrong anyway," Noah said. "'96 Geo Metro says working class upbringing."

"You're both right." She let her fingers rest on my forearm for an entire microsecond. "My dad's a minister over in

Dormont. Have you seen *7th Heaven*? That's pretty much my life except I only have one younger brother, not seventeen."

"A paper about *7th Heaven* and gender politics is just waiting to be written." Oz pulled out his iPhone and tapped a reminder. "Something like *Late '90s Female Subservience: The Domination of Femininity as Depicted in 7th* Heaven *and Other WB Sitcoms.*"

Sloan rubbed the back of his shoulder and told him it was a fine idea. We nodded our heads. We listened to the low-pitched death-wail of twenty-first century indie rock. We toasted my birthday and the furious lyrics of my favorite rapper Kanye West. This was America. This was why my grandfather had fought in World War II. This was how I spent my twenty-fifth birthday.

We settled up at one-thirty and headed our separate ways. Oz, who usually walked home with me, decided to go to an all night coffee shop, claiming he wanted to brush up on an ur-text in the field of post-Marx, pre-Benjamin Marxist theory. My apartment was only seven blocks away, but I lingered outside the Cage, not ready to let my birthday slip by, contemplating hitting one of the other Squirrel Hill bars for a solitary toast. But then I heard the sputtering of an engine block that wouldn't start. I spent so many days of my childhood in my dad's body shop that I'd recognize that whiny revving followed by clicking anywhere.

It came from a parked Geo Metro across the street, and it didn't take long for me to put two and two together. Ivy Chase. In distress. I crossed the street and knocked on her window. She looked up and smiled with a tilt of her head.

"I thought you were saying all that shit about your car just to keep up with the big boys," I said.

She gave her shoulders a shrug and blew at her bangs. "One thing you'll learn about me is I'm as sincere as a modern girl gets."

I leaned my elbow against the door. I was pretty drunk and trying to use that to my advantage, to appear playful and charming, the living definition of a good time. "Did you try giving it a little gas?"

"Yeah. But old Flannery does this all the time."

"Flannery?"

"Don't make fun."

A pause. I didn't want to seem too anxious or anything. I looked across the street like there was something very important I needed to take care of, perhaps a supermodel who desperately needed my penis spelunking around inside of her.

"It's no big deal," Ivy said. "I'll call Triple-A. I've done it a million times."

"At one in the morning?"

She kept smiling. Her eyes shone beneath the streetlights and I was filled with the urge to bend over and kiss each of her eyelids.

"Well, old man, what's your solution?"

"I live a few blocks that way." I pointed in a vague direction. "I could give you a lift."

A bus rumbled by on the other side of the street, an oddity at this time of night.

"You all right to drive?" Ivy asked.

"Driving is my middle name. My parents had it narrowed down to that or Chainsaw. Michael Chainsaw Bishop."

"You try really hard, huh?"

"Trying is my middle name."

We piled into my Saturn at the other end of Squirrel Hill. I started the engine and, feeling brave, set my iPod to random.

Usually, when I first take a girl in my car, I spend a lot of time thinking about how I should expose her to my musical tastes. Should I go with something soulful and old to tell her I'm deep? Or shiny and futuristic to signal I'm not only playful, but oh so hip.

The iPod cycled to Orson Welles' *War of the Worlds* broadcast. I tried to skip tracks, but Ivy snatched the iPod from the dashboard and shook her head.

"Really?" she asked.

"Yeah, well, I'm kind of reading an Orson Welles biography and thought it'd be interesting."

So we listened to Orson Welles while I drove, and even though I enjoyed *Citizen Kane, The Magnificent Ambersons*, even *The Lady from Shanghai*, I just couldn't get used to the pitch of his voice. There was something alien in it, otherworldly, and I thought maybe this was the source of his early success, his twenty-something stardom. Maybe all that talent originated in his irregular voice box, genius spreading to his extremities like liquid warmth.

"You know what his last performance was before he died?" I asked.

Ivy kept scrolling through my iPod, no doubt judging me based on what music I had and had not transferred to the device. "What?"

"*Transformers: The Animated Movie*. He voiced Unicron. His final interviewer asked what the film was like and he said it was about children's toys who did terrible things to each other. Can you believe that?"

"Believe what?"

"Guy made *Citizen Kane* and died voicing a giant robot that eats planets. F. Scott was right. There really are no second acts."

"Uh-huh."

I merged onto the highway and wiped the sweat off the back of my neck. I was losing her, laying it on too thick, too clever. Ivy played an old Pixies song about gouging out eyeballs.

"You know what I always think about whenever I watch something from the fifties or before?" she asked.

Ok, ok. I could work with this. "What do you think about?"

"Their voices sound so different than ours. Think of any black and white movie. The men sound deeper. The women sound so much more proper. I think our voices have fundamentally changed."

"How would that happen?"

She looked out the window. "Oh, I don't know. All the typical answers. Radiation. The internet. Loss of faith."

We came upon the city skyline, towering and bright beyond a bend on the highway, all those well-lit yellow bridges Pittsburgh was famous for. I only had a little more time before we'd arrive in Dormont where she lived. "So, what do you do? For work I mean."

"I'm doing PR for my father's church, designing flyers, setting up radio spots, banner ads," she said. "I majored in PR at Fordham. Minored in English."

"I minored in English too. Who do you read?"

"Pretty much everyone." She started talking faster. "Right now I'm kind of obsessed with Flannery O' Connor. You a fan?"

We drove through the Fort Pitt Tunnel, nothing but flashing yellow lights reminding me of a gazillion sci-fi films, all those elaborate starfighter bays. As for Flannery? Well, I've always considered her a technical master. She can weave a plot; she can make things surprising and inevitable all at once. But I'm troubled by her obsession with morality in the simplest of terms and her over the top endings where characters are impaled by icicles or struck down with heart attacks.

"I absolutely adore her," I said.

"Really? My boyfriend thinks she's a women's writer."

Boyfriend.

I was old enough—twenty-five!—to know how to act when a girl mentions the dreaded b word. As a younger man, I would have picked at the guy's weaknesses, maybe make him seem like a total douche bag in comparison to moi— *Oh, your boyfriend went bar hopping last night? That's cool. I was out volunteering with orphans, you know, taking them to the aquarium to look at giant squids.*—but now, I understood the only way to subvert a boyfriend was a precise mixture of compliments and indifference. The girl would think I was mature, and when the boyfriend grew jealous, she'd subconsciously be drawn toward my natural confidence and goodwill.

"What's your boyfriend do?"

"He's a carpenter in New York City. I met him when I was at Fordham. He dropped out of college, but he's pretty much the smartest guy I ever met. All self taught. He's read Joyce, Aristotle, Marx, you name it."

"That's pretty impressive."

"It is."

On the other side of the tunnel, everything urban gave way to the winding roads and wilderness of Western Pennsylvania. It always amazed me how in Pittsburgh you'd be surrounded by city one minute—the endless pedestrians, violinists performing on corners, the low buzz of bars— and the next you'd be in bumblefuck, nothing but trees and mountains and elk lodges. The sudden shift turned us silent and we listened to the Pixies sing about the end of the world. The song was twenty years old and everyone was still waiting for it to happen.

Ivy lived in a development on the outer edge of Dormont, a small neighborhood with a still intact Main Street, all barbershops and Polish restaurants hocking halušky for five dollars. Every house looked the same—brick, two stories, a white garage and a small patch of grass. I idled beside her lawn, reluctant to pull into the driveway as if the house held some kind of power over me. It was well past two and a light shone behind a second floor window, the curtain swaying menacingly.

I cleared my throat. "You going to be able to get your car tomorrow?"

"Sure. My dad will drive me in." She thanked me for the ride, leaned across the shifter and gave me a hug. I clasped my hands against the small of her back, that wonderful sweet spot that made me want to sit there forever listening to the Pixies while holding this girl, all curves and blonde bangs. She fumbled with the door lock, stepped out, and I panicked that I was letting yet another human opportunity slip through my fingers. The stereo cackled as the song ended.

"Hey, Ivy!"

She turned back and ducked her head through the open window.

"You know, I was thinking, since you haven't lived in Pittsburgh since high school you might not know too many people. Maybe we can go sightseeing sometime? Maybe grab a few drinks or something?"

She smiled and looked surprised, even pleased. "That might be ok. Ask Sloan for my number. Happy birthday, Michael."

And then Ivy Chase was gone, up the driveway and into her house. I sat there looking through the windshield at the lit second floor. Something about her home—how the walls just barely contained the overwhelming humanity of Ivy Chase and her family inside—filled me with a sharp fear like nothing I'd experienced since the yellow days of my childhood. A minute passed and the light went out, replaced by another at the opposite end of the house, presumably Ivy preparing for bed. I put the car in drive and left the development, a feeling in my stomach something like dread.

The Oh So Imperfect

On the Monday morning after my birthday, I slipped in to my third-floor cubicle and did what I always did for the first twenty minutes of work: I opened up a random e-mail and furrowed my brow, stroked my chin, did anything to look smart, hard-working and absorbed, the model twenty-something go getter of a nebulous corporate entity. It was appropriate on this day so close to the anniversary of my birth to ruminate on my glorious past. As a one time boy of strict Catholic origins, I once believed in my heart of hearts that the Lord and Savior—the baby Jesus Christ—had placed me on this earth for two specific and beautiful reasons. I was either going to become the greatest video game designer in the history of the universe or the greatest comic book writer in the history of the universe. By my late-teens, both of these interests had waned considerably. I held onto my collection of 2D adventures for the Nintendo Entertainment System, and once a month I'd trek down to the comic shop for doses of *Ultimate Spider-Man* and *The Walking Dead*. But dreams of following the paths of those worshipped creators from my youth had expired like the curdled milk in my dorm room mini-fridge. What stayed with me was a sense of entitlement, that my life was truly meaningful, that I had the potential to do something wonderful and unusual. Like the vast majority of my peers, I'd yet to discover exactly what that could be.

So at twenty-five I found myself making twelve dollars an hour at Digital Deluxe in the franchise laden Southside of Pittsburgh. My title was AFQCELE, or Audio Fidelity Quality Control English Language Editor. My work was located in an office park that on one side faced a river and shoppers patrolling an outlet mall, and on the other, a swooping highway. As a cubicle-monkey, my view was confined to a lone Dilbert calendar, an ironic gift from Oz that my co-workers took at face value, commenting on whatever zany mishap old Dilbert had gotten himself into that month. We specialized in DVD coding and production. I was the only person who proofread the subtitles that had already been completed on the cheap in Mexico. They needed me to correct colloquialisms and other human errors. So I sat four corners with IT specialists who spent their days singing the praises of Linux and open source versions of Twitter, Facebook and Microsoft Word. On Wednesdays we received free bagels from BagelHut.

Ten new Proof Ones were waiting for me that morning: seven featurettes for the *Lipstick Jungle Season Two* DVD, the full length *How To Lose a Guy in Ten Days* Deluxe Edition, and two episodes of the short lived *Dana Carey Show* from 1996. I tucked my hair behind my ears and slid on my headphones. They pressed the plastic of my glasses hard against my skull, and within an hour, I'd inevitably have to shift them, maybe remove my glasses altogether and squint at the little video box on my screen. I started the first featurette and hovered my finger just above the mouse, ready to pause the tape if anything looked amiss, Michael Bishop the only force between a misplaced comma and the unassuming public. I had the only job I knew of where watching eight hours of television a day was mandatory. I was pretty sure this much media consumption had melted my brain.

> Brooke Shields: Welcome to the set of Lipstick Jungle. I thought I'd take you guys behind the scenes for a sneak peak of NBC's hottest show!

I paused the clip. The Mexicans had forgotten to italicize *Lipstick Jungle*, misspelled the word peek, and inserted a superfluous exclamation point. I opened up a webpage on Digital's servers and suggested the changes in three separate boxes—I didn't have the power to manually alter the subtitles myself. By eleven, I'd finished the featurettes and decided to reward myself with some internet trolling. I checked gmail. One new message on the web comic. I clicked over, scrolled to the bottom of the page and found this gem from one of my 200 subscribers:

Lasandra Prochaska *says*:
January 11, 2008 at 10:37 am

Satisfy your grrl with the most glorious boner of yur lifetime. Make yourself thicker and loOoOnger today. Click here.

I wondered whether or not Lasandra Prochaska was real, if she was some Russian peasant from the world of Chekhov, if she sat at home in a beige housedress furiously leaving penis enlargement ads all over the internet. More likely, she was a bot created by some zit-addled hacker, lines of code with human qualities that discharged spyware like pollination. My dearest Lasandra!

Before I could exit out of the browser, I heard a woman clear her throat behind me. I spun around and gave the office secretary my smarmiest grin. She was Polish with wonderfully wide hips, a little too much makeup. Maybe a year younger than me and always wearing these horrendous boots that came up to her knees. Junie Censulla. Rumor had it she'd let Mr. Tarryton, the suave divorcee who worked in Client Relations, pleasure her with a jumbo sharpie in the handicapped stall. She smacked her gum and cocked a hand on her hip.

"Mr. Hudelson would like to see you in his office, Michael."

"Oh. Oh. Mm."

Mr. Hudelson wasn't my boss exactly, but I still buttoned up my shirt and patted down my hair before entering his office, a glass enclosure with that nice river view I so coveted. My actual boss was a woman I had never met from Bangladesh. Madhuri Bahl and I conferenced on Skype once a week and discussed the stalemate of my war against Oxford commas and misuses of there, their and they're. Pittsburgh only hired me as a tentative first step toward developing a full-blown subtitling division. During training, they'd promised to hire me a partner within six weeks, a team within the year. Forty months in and I was still utterly alone.

I stood in the doorway of Hudelson's office. Framed posters hung from the walls. Famous concert shots of the Beatles, the Clash, the Who, and the Rolling Stones. It was well known throughout the office that before Hudelson joined the world of corporate America he'd helmed some semi-popular band that had ruled over the Pittsburgh bar scene with an iron fist. It was hard to imagine twenty years removed. These days, Hudelson resembled a goofier, middle class Lex Luthor, bald and trim in a baggy gray suit.

"Michael." He followed my eyes to the Stones poster. "You like the Stones, kid? One time I opened for the drummer,

Charlie Watts. He came through town promoting one of his solo projects. It was a killer show."

I forced a smile. We'd all heard this story a thousand times. Hudelson unleashed it at least once a week on some unsuspecting new employee, or even worse, a veteran who knew the details by heart.

My chair was at least four inches lower than his and I felt like I'd once again been called to Sister Donna's office in grade school for mouthing off, that crucifix behind her, a golden Jesus frozen in orgasmic agony.

"Did Junie tell you what this was all about?" he asked.

"No."

A tour boat chugged downriver and I wondered what type of fat cats enjoyed the waters of Pittsburgh on a Monday in January? Did they wear monocles? Did they own top hats? I couldn't see them, but I despised them regardless.

"Of course she didn't. Well, I never took you for a dummy, Michael. You can see the writing on the walls. I'm sure you knew this was coming."

I nodded, my stomach clenching as I realized I was being "let go," a euphemism every bit as phony as "friendly fire." Digital Deluxe was my first real job. I'd worked KB Toys in high school, Target during college. And I'd excelled! I'd sold more batteries than anyone! I was the Ray Charles of cash registers! I glared at Hudelson and refrained from hurling my cell phone at his face. Cocksucker. Stupid baby boomers. They hogged all the good jobs and saddled Generation X with the service industry, left Generation Facebook global warming and an overpopulation crisis. Fucking d-bags. They'd partied it up at Woodstock and San Francisco. Got fat off the government and soon they'd cripple Social Security and leave me eating ramen noodles for the rest of my life, listening to Kanye West on a Martian old folks' home with other fogies who spoke wistfully for days when the internet was contained to screens. I eyed the pencils in his

Tiger Woods mug. I could grab one and stab Hudelson in the eye, an explosion of blood and gore. I could ninja flip over him and karate chop through the window, maybe land in a garbage truck and shoot the bird at the office, the whole place exploding like in an action flick. I'd ride that truck to Mexico and become a traveling gaucho singer. If that didn't work, I could hunt down the Mexican subtitle editors and teach them a thing or two about company policy on exclamation points, show them the definitive spelling of till while I pulverized their fingertips in a rusty vice.

Fucking baby boomers!

"Michael. All signs are heading for the big r. Recession. And I don't know if you've noticed, but we haven't exactly staffed our subtitling department. I'm not saying we're going to can the division just yet. That's not what this little meeting is about. But it's a possibility. A very real possibility. It's something I've discussed with corporate. It's not up to me or anything like that. I don't have that kind of leverage. If I did, well, I'd never do anything to hurt you, Michael. You're a clever guy. If we axe the division here, they might offer you a spot in Bangladesh or something. I hear it's really gentrifying."

Bangladesh. What did I know about Bangladesh? "Sir, I don't think I'd like that."

His face turned grave, his domed head porcelain under the pallid lights. "Well that's not very good. That's not very good at all. But I'll tell you what. I'll keep you posted. I'll keep you abreast of our developing situation here. And we'll be following your output very closely, not me, but corporate. You understand. In the meantime, I'd think about some alternative career options. I hear the American Eagle Headquarters down the block is looking for some up and comers."

I fantasized about quitting right then and there, about going all berserker rage on his ass, but instead I thanked him for his honesty and hurried away. I was sweating and practically jogged to Noah's office. I banged on the door and found him in the dark, staring at the glow of his computer screen, his iPod buds tucked into his ears. He'd framed posters of basketball squads on the walls. The Jordan-era Bulls. The Kobe/Shaq Lakers. Noah was the only person I'd ever met who cheered for an entire league, not just one team in particular.

I asked him to get destroyed with me after work. He flashed two thumbs up.

That night we hit up the Library, a bar by Digital Deluxe where everything was named after books and famous authors—"Yeah, I'll have *The Old Man and the Sea*." Translation: fish and chips. The Southside was not a good place for Noah Black and me to work. It was home to East Carson Street, a compact strip more densely packed with bars than any other block in America. The two of us could walk there every day after work if we wanted, the occasional happy hour pitcher transforming into last call jager bombs with flirty bartenders. We were a people prone to excess. Our fathers, and in some cases even our grandfathers, had sent men to the moon, had tested the limits of human achievement. We no longer understood the meaning of the word "limit." We wanted to get hammered and talk about Hitchcock references on *The Simpsons* until the polar ice caps melted and drowned us in our collective madness.

We drank John Irvings at the bar while I explained my run in with Hudelson. The Library smelled like the musk of the old novels I'd once discovered in my grandmother's attic, all science fiction and noir, a fragrance I would buy in cologne form if only some conglomerate had the cojones to produce it. Noah nodded his head from time to time, his

eyes wandering to the familiar scroll of *SportsCenter* overhead.

"And then," I told him, "I pulled out my Glock and blew
the old bastard's brains out."

"Mm-hmm." Noah munched on pretzels.

"All right, what's going on?"

He signaled the bartender for two Carvers and kept his
gaze on the television. "So I kind of cheated on Sloan again."

I tipped my glass to my lips and gave myself time to
think. I'd known about Noah's infidelities for years and had
even witnessed a few myself. When I first started at Digital
Deluxe, we got shitfaced every night of the week. One time
we ended up at the Holiday Inn and introduced ourselves
to two mothers from Philly in town for their kids' soccer
tournament. They looked late-thirties and weren't especially
attractive, nowhere near as pretty as Sloan or the handful of
girls I'd dated in college. While their children slept soundly
two floors above, the mothers made out with us right there
at the abandoned hotel bar, the gentle vocal stylings of Elton
John tickling our eardrums.

I thought that would be the end of things, but every once
in awhile we'd both get too drunk after work and roll up on
girls, Noah sometimes going home with one. That hadn't
happened in over a year and I'd thought things had changed,
that maybe when Noah moved in with Sloan he'd given up
the allure of easily seduced women. I'd never told Sloan any
of this and understood it was a breach of her trust, that I'd
known her for years, that I owed her at the very least the
truth. But Noah was in so many ways the type of friend I'd
always wanted, the bro who could explain sports to me, the
compadre who wouldn't back down from a fight, the buddy
who would toss back drink after drink until last call. I idol-
ized him to be sure, but buzzed in the Library, I knew that
wasn't the whole truth, that deep down I was relieved each
and every time Noah cheated because of what it signified:

that he and Sloan weren't serious, that one day Oz and Sloan and I could return to the three musketeers mentality that had been our status quo throughout college. Sloan Smith. It was difficult imagining anyone worthy of her.

"Who was it?" I asked, the disgust in my tone unmistakable.

"*She*. Not it."

"Never can be sure with your taste in women."

"Do you have to turn everything into a joke?"

I ordered two Faulkners, my attempt at apology. "All right, go on."

"It happened after your birthday. We were driving home and got into it. Sloan said I never let her talk when we went out and I said that was bullshit. One of those little fights that's totally meaningless, you know? But it really blew up once we got back to the apartment and I just got the hell out of there, jumped in the car, headed to the after hours club. The Castle? Ran into Junie. We got to talking. You know how things go."

"Shit. Junie the secretary Junie? Did you stay over?"

"Yeah."

"What did you tell Sloan?"

"She was furious, but I told her I drove to your place and stayed on the futon."

"Are you going to hook up with Junie again? You see her every day."

"No." He slammed back the Faulkner. "I don't know."

We sat in silence. The Library was filling up now that the Happy Hour specials had kicked in, the servers whizzing around the tables in the back dining room. Noah Black and Junie Censulla.

"You still love Sloan?"

"That counting thing she does on the internet really freaks me out." Another handful of pretzels. "But yeah. Sure I do."

"Does your family still want you to settle down?"

"Oh, hell yeah. Every time I go over for dinner it's engagement this, wedding that. My two older brothers, they're both married. Oldest has a kid on the way. They're old school Pittsburghers, you know? Thrilled I found a local girl. Hated the chicks I dated in college. And I really love Sloan. I'm not going to find anyone better suited for me. Maybe I'll stop being attracted to other women once we're married, once she pops out a kid or something." He finished his drink and called for the tab. "I bought an engagement ring, Michael. A fucking engagement ring and I'm screwing Junie Censulla."

This was as big a show of Noah Black's indecisive side as I'd ever seen. He was usually so certain. Three nights a week he coached a biddy basketball team at the YMCA, and on Sundays he uploaded videos to YouTube teaching lay ups, explaining how to drive to the lane, setting an example for the perfect free throw form. He exuded confidence. It didn't matter that he had less than a hundred subscribers. It didn't matter that his girlfriend had managed to surpass him merely by counting, that every day his prospects of opening up a basketball camp seemed dimmer. He was Noah Black.

We left and waited under an awning for the bus. It had started raining, the city cold and gray, the pollution from our forefathers still turning everything to dust and depression. Even through the haze we could make out the yellow bridges by downtown, a tinge of otherworldliness in a city of steel. The bus arrived and we found seats by some kids eating snacks out of grocery bags, and suddenly I began to feel something light and airy glowing behind my chest, the hot breath of contentment. I sat on the aisle, Noah by the window. I wanted to tell him all about Ivy Chase. How I'd driven her home and she'd agreed to hang out with me soon. That I was completely, totally, 200 percent infatuated with this local beauty returned to us from the hobo dirt and skyscraper grime of New York City. The bus rattled over a bridge and

I kept my mouth shut. I was not blind to Noah's doubt and pain. I pictured the engagement ring lurking in his pocket, pulsating an SOS, a warning for us all: the heavyhearted, the young, the oh so imperfect.

The Age of Anxiety, Fear & Indecision (Part 1 of 3)

The Childhood of Michael Bishop

I was six. School had just let out for summer. I sat in the backseat of my parents' station wagon reading an issue of *Amazing Spider-Man*. Doctor Octopus had gotten the better of the friendly neighborhood wall crawler and was about to deliver the killing blow with one of his terrible robot arms. I don't remember where we were headed, but Dad drove while Mom hummed along to a Monkees cassette on the stereo. We were at the end of Route 6, a four-lane road that leads out of Scranton up into the mountains, franchise restaurants on either side, infinite off-brand department stores. When the road ends, the right lane takes a ninety-degree turn down into side streets while the left shoots forward into the wilderness. People in the right lane who want to go straight are presented with a choice: they either come to a complete stop and wait to merge, or they speed up and try to overtake the passing lane. The grass alongside is littered with wreaths and burned out candles standing in for the Scrantonian dead.

We were in the left lane, about thirty yards away from the end of Route 6, when a white van appeared on our right. My mother told my father to slow down, to let the jerk in. I wasn't concerned. My parents were there. I was safe. But my father refused to back down and neither did the van, smooth as a cloud over a summer barbeque. The right lane veered into the suburbs. The van hurtled forward on the warning track. My mother screamed. The van slammed into the passenger side, the sheet metal crumpling like snapped bone. We careened into the oncoming lane and clipped the back end of an Oldsmobile. My body lurched forward. My face smashed into the headrest. Something mechanical hissed and the stereo stopped dead before springing back to life five seconds later, the happy dumb voices of the Monkees. I looked down at my comic. Spider-Man was nonplussed.

No one died. This is not a story of deceased parents. My father broke his wrist, my mother got a lifelong limp, and I escaped with a cast on my arm that made a normal summer full of play and other children impossible. In an attempt to salvage the dwindling season my parents purchased me a brand spanking new Nintendo Entertainment System.

That was a moment I would never be able to forget, maybe even more so than the accident itself. The Nintendo Entertainment System came in a large cardboard box decorated by the stars and emptiness of outer space. The system towered in the middle, all boxy and gray, my plastic portal to other worlds. It was the size of a VCR with a plastic flap on the front where you could fit sandwich-sized games. And the wires! So many wires. Wires for as far as the eye could see. I'd be remiss not to mention the Nintendo Zapper, that phallic red and gray gun that stole millions of boys' imaginations.

Receiving the Nintendo Entertainment System was the happiest moment of my life, a trillion times better than losing my virginity years later.

The games were so flat then, two-dimensional, primitive-looking. Cartoon Super Mario barely looked human, required an active imagination, was only a step above the archaic visuals of *Pong*. If you've only casually played video games, then you can't truly comprehend the inner depths of their joys. You don't know what it feels like to give yourself up so completely to another you, a better version of yourself. You become the avatar. Super Mario, an Italian plumber tumbled through the looking glass. Link, the boy knight on a magical crusade to rescue Princess Zelda from the terrible Ganon. Samus Aran, the intergalactic bounty hunter tracking down alien eggs on a world ruled by Mother Brain. When you are represented by an avatar, you are no longer Michael Bishop, a skinny boy with a broken arm and sharp ribs that push against your polar bear t-shirt. You are not weak and loathsome and eternally frightened that some threat lurks around every corner existing only to dismember you.

That summer I played and played and played, and over time, this electronic world of bright colors and sprites began to feel safer, realer, better than the actual world I knew, an unpredictable place where a crazed van could send my whole being into a tailspin. In *Super Mario Brothers*, there was repetition and safety. The enemies always appeared in exactly the same place responding in exactly the same way. I lost myself in those games for hours at a time, refused to leave the safety of my house and instead began my descent into microchips and immateriality. I feared forests and lakes and birds and wind and most of all people.

The digital!

My first true love!

The Final Resident of
a Post-Human Earth

A week after my birthday, I received my first text message from Ivy Chase asking to hang out. We went for pizza at Church Brew Works, a protestant church remodeled into a microbrewery. We caught *Dr. Strangelove* at the indie movie theatre. Soon, we were meeting up every other day. But it didn't feel like I'd made any significant progress until we went bowling.

I took her to Forward Lanes, a tiny alley above a bar in my neighborhood, perennially empty but with awesome specials. We exchanged our stylish sneakers for those greasy lane shoes and away we went, Ivy dazzling with a purple handkerchief around her neck. She threw three strikes in the first three frames while I barely managed to knock down ten pins.

I waited by the ball return. "Bowling. You're good at bowling. Who are you?"

Ivy looked up from the score sheet. "I was on the team in high school."

"You must have been the biggest nerd of all time."

"Teapot meet kettle."

I lifted my twelve ball and heaved it down the lane. It knocked down a single pin, a second wobbling ever so slightly in its wake.

"So, is your boyfriend a good bowler?" I joined her at the plastic table.

"I don't know. We never actually went back in New York."

"Yeah?" I watched her walk toward her ball. "How long did you guys go out?"

"Two months."

Two months? Two months was nothing! Surely, I was the luckiest boy in Pittsburgh, nay, the luckiest boy in America. There I was with a beautiful blonde who'd only had a boyfriend of two measly months. There we were, the two of us, alive!

She threw another strike. "Yeah, well," I said, "Italians are notoriously bad at bowling any way."

"I was thinking about that. Your last name. Bishop. It's not very Italian. And you're pretty pale. Where's the chest hair? Where's the Guido windbreaker?"

She didn't hurry me back to the lane. I was winning her over, could feel it in my bones. I smiled and leaned closer. "I'm pretty much the worst Italian of all time. My Mom's half-German so I guess I take after her. All I need is to marry some Japanese anime chick and I'll have the perfect Axis Power baby. Nieder mit den Verbündeten!"

"So that explains the gawky demeanor and porcelain complexion." She touched my forearm. "But what about the last name?"

I kept grinning. Just like the Axis Power joke, I'd told this story many times. Rehearsed and pitch-perfect, it lacked all the quiet risks of spontaneity. I knew it made me look interesting, unique, that I was worthy of a girl like Ivy's attention. I gave her my very best imitation of earnestness.

"When my great-grandfather moved here from Italy, we were the Bianchis. His daughter changed the name, my grandmother. She was born in Scranton but decided to head out west. Wanted to be an actress. So Layla Bianchi became Lily Bishop. Changed her birthday to the Fourth of July and everything. She wanted to get rid of every last inch of her heritage."

"How'd that work out for old Lily Bishop?"

I shrugged and stood by the lane. "Grandma? She did a few voiceovers during the War, nothing major. Mostly she waited tables. She came back to Scranton two years later and married her high school sweetheart, a full-blooded German. She made him take her last name. Now she prays a lot and watches CNN."

When I looked back, Ivy was smiling, not her trademark smirk, but something genuine, something honest. There was a goodness inside of her, a purity that was so rare in women I considered hip, women who liked the Pixies and retro movie theatres and LookAtThisFuckingHipster.com. She lacked the trademark nihilism, and I selfishly wanted to absorb her best qualities and become that good and decent person Sloan so often told me I was at my inner most depths.

We finished our frame and sat at a table in the back finishing the last of our beers. A kind of sadness gurgled in my easily agitated stomach. It was almost time to go. Usually, I looked forward to the end of dates. I prided myself on making a favorable impression and then getting out of there as quickly as possible before I could ruin things with one of the many stupid comments just waiting on the tip of my tongue. But with Ivy, things were different. I actually enjoyed spending time with her and didn't want our outings to end. Something about her drew me out, my true self, the way I felt around my closest friends guzzling beers on the second floor of the Squirrel Cage.

"So New York," I said. "What was that like?"

"It was great," she said almost breathlessly. "I loved Manhattan. There was so much to do, and all these people, and it wasn't the traditional college experience at all. It was much more adult. The whole city was our campus, you know? I got to discover all these bands and quirky coffee shops and cool little improv shows. It was nonstop, just totally nonstop." She finished her beer. "But I missed Pittsburgh. It's small but not too small. It's lovable. The people here are so down to earth and kind, and I really love my family. That's me in a nutshell. Manhattan and Pittsburgh. I'm a living contradiction. On one hand, I'm trying to be this really hip, modern girl. But on the other, I'm the same sincere kid who cried for a week when the Steelers lost Super Bowl XXX."

"What's the more dominant side? Pittsburgh or Manhattan?"

She smirked and shook her head. "I'm not going to have to tell you everything, am I?"

I scooped up our beers and tossed them in the trash. I watched Ivy fiddle with something in her purse, her eyebrows scrunched in concentration. There we were. Happy. Together.

During this fabled time of getting to know Ivy better, I endured one of my monthly phone calls with my Scrantonian parents. They asked what I was eating, how much I was drinking, how work was going, etc. etc. I imagined them inside the home where I'd grown up pacing back and forth with a clipboard, filling in how many bananas I consumed each month, how many Yuenglings. Maybe they had a chart tracking my rate of consumption ever since I first packed my belongings into a rental van and headed west for the great unknown of Pittsburgh, a city that at first glance seemed like a larger Scranton, a Scranton on overdrive.

To the untrained eye, the architecture in Scranton is very similar to Pittsburgh's. The same abandoned smokestacks, the same brick houses and crumbling hills, all the tropes of an early-twentieth century working class haven turned rust belt disaster area. But the difference is that Pittsburgh reclaimed its origins. Its blight has been updated, remodeled, made chic. Empty churches have been transformed into community centers. Factories have become spaciously hip lofts. The waterfront has been reimagined into the Waterfront, a massive shopping center complete with a movie theatre, Starbucks and Target. Pittsburgh is Archie Bunker: so working-class it's cool.

Scranton is none of these things. Despite being the first city in the country to have a working trolley system, and the fact that it's located over an ocean of coal, Scranton never reached the heights Pittsburgh did during the industrial heyday of World War II, and unfortunately, Scranton fell a lot further in the ensuing aftermath—figuratively and literally as many sections of the town are actually sinking into the old mines. The streets are cracked, ex-cons run for mayor, and the city has been bankrupt ever since Hitler blew his brains out in the Führerbunker. The same blight that existed in my parents' day blooms today. In short, there is nothing hip about Scranton, Pennsylvania with the exception of NBC's *The Office*, set in my hometown but filmed in California landscapes so remote, so beautiful and sunny, that it might as well take place on another planet according to actual residents.

As per usual, the conversation circled around to my love life. My parents, especially my limp-saddled mother, made no secret that they thought twenty-five was too old to be single, and wasn't it time I found a nice, preferably Italian, girl to take care of me? My father was an auto-body man, had taken over his father's shop after his death. My mother was a manager at a credit card call center that overlooked a ski resort. They wanted to leave Scranton but never did and were glad that I had managed to escape with a job. The only thing I needed now was a wife.

"There is this new kind of, sort of girl I'm maybe seeing. Her name is Ivy."

My mother shrieked. "Ivy? Ivy. What a pretty name. I bet she's beautiful. You hear that Mike?"

She was calling out for my father, my namesake, no doubt on the other side of the living room delivering a vigorous fondling to the family beagle. "Ivy. Nice," I heard him shout.

"Tell me more," Mom went on. "What's she like? Where's she from? What does she do?"

"Oh, I don't know. You know. The usual things." I sat down in front of my computer. "I'll just send you a link to her Facebook page, ok?"

"What? No. That's weird. Don't do that."

My mother's timid entrance into the world of the digital, the world of Facebook, involved posting a single picture of her precious beagle. The idea that she would actually look at a prospective girlfriend's profile was laughable, but I brought up Ivy's profile anyway. We were meeting again the next day, a harmless romp in the zoo, and I wondered if there was some secret knowledge waiting for me in her profile, some tiny nugget I'd glossed over before, some trinket that would allow me to take things to the next level in a manner not unlike the hidden warp pipes scattered throughout all those Super Mario games of my youth. I loaded her page and studied.

Ivy Chase is drinking chai w/her father in the den.

Basic Information

Networks:	Fordham Alum '08
	New York, NY
	Pittsburgh, PA
Sex:	Female
Birthday:	January 10
Hometown:	Pittsburgh, PA
Relationship Status:	In a Relationship with Tommy Mendocino
Looking For:	Networking
Political Views:	Moderate
Religious Views:	God is Love

Personal Information

Interests:	Art, fiction, poetry, beauty, Public Relations, Tommy Mendocino, rediscovering Pittsburgh after an extended absence
Favorite Music:	Too many to list. Right now: Neutral Milk Hotel, Belle & Sebastian, Kate Nash, Stars, Vampire Weekend, M.I.A., the Pixies
Favorite TV Shows:	LOST
Favorite Books:	So many... A Good Man is Hard to Find, Everything That Rises Must Converge, Our Town, The Progress of Love, Shiloh and Other Stories, Winesburg Ohio, The Safety of Objects, Franny and Zooey
About Me:	Forever in my prayers, DLC.

Forever in my prayers, DLC. What did that mean? I stared. I squinted. I touched the words on the screen.

"Hello? Michael? Are you there?" my mom asked.

"Yeah. Hey. I'm going to have to call you back."

I awoke the next morning to discover that Pittsburgh had entered a rare, out-of-season warming. Forty degrees! Ivy wore a turtleneck! Only one coat for me! We drove into the tunnel that connected Dormont to the city and zoo, but when we emerged on the other side the sky had erupted. Fat beads of water exploded against the windshield. I cursed under my breath. I didn't want a soggy day ruining my chances with Ivy.

"Ugh," she moaned.

I drove slower. The turn off to my apartment came up on my right. "You want to head to my place? Maybe order Chinese or something?"

She nodded, so I took the off ramp. In the short time it took us to run inside, we both got ourselves drenched. I put towels around our shoulders and made coffee. We sat on the couch, a lumpy relic left behind by the previous tenants. We watched *The Simpsons* on mute. Oz was at Pitt's campus I was sure, locked away in the Cathedral of Learning, trying to order everyday chaos into zeroes and ones.

"So," I said.

"So."

The rain beat on the tin awning over the porch and made a kind of music. She shivered a little so I patted her shoulder. It felt fleshy in my palm, bigger than I'd expected somehow. More alive.

"Let me ask you something." I kept my eyes on the television, on Homer Simpson falling down a mountainside and screaming *D'oh*. "I was looking at your Facebook profile. 'Forever in my prayers, DLC.' What's that mean?"

She didn't look at me. "It's just something from when I was younger."

"You want to talk about it?"

"It's not something I share with everyone."

I squeezed her shoulder. "You can tell me."

She smiled and began, and it took everything in my

power not to show how eager I was over this victory. I understood what this meant, that Ivy trusted me enough to tell me
something important and potentially revealing about her
true character. That our relationship, whatever it was, had
evolved beyond the surface of everyday human interaction.

"Danielle Lauren Caviletti. She was my best friend growing up. She lived next-door and we went to the same grade
school. The same high school. We used to practice kissing in
her older brother's tree house."

"Super hot."

She shook her head. "I know you have some kind of problem where you have to turn everything into a joke, and it's
endearing, it really is. But not this, ok?"

I said I was sorry. I'd hidden behind sarcasm and decay-
ing Nintendo games for so very long. But humans—or at
least Michael Bishop—cannot fight their true nature.

"So we were best friends and we're totally inseparable
and make plans to go to college together, dorm in New York,
be each other's maids of honor. All that." Ivy turned back to
the television. A CGI gecko danced around a sombrero in an
auto insurance ad. "So it's summer vacation after ninth grade
and I get a call from her mother, which is strange because
they're on vacation to Ocean City. They went there every
year. Got in the family van and drove eight hours or something to barbeque on a crowded beach and swim in seaweed.
But her mom talks to my mom who talks to my dad and I
know something's up because they're all acting really weird.
You know how kids can sense these things sometimes?"

"Yes." It took all I had to keep my voice from trembling.

"So my dad," she said, "he takes me aside and tells me
with absolutely zero buildup that Danielle's in heaven. She
swam out too far in the ocean and got pulled in by the under-
tow. Lifeguards couldn't reach her in time."

My infatuation with Ivy Chase had been growing and
growing ever since I first spotted her entering the Squirrel

Cage on my birthday. But this revelation was the kicker: a trauma that reflected my own. I knew I should have told her right then about Keith Tedesco. But I couldn't. I could barely move. We locked eyes. I saw myself.

Ivy pointed weakly at the television. "My boyfriend loves *Family Guy*," she said.

We were still soaking wet, our coffee losing steam, and what I remember most about that first kiss is thinking how much I hated that show, how awesome it was when it debuted in 1999 and how quickly it jumped the shark when it was resurrected from cancellation, how *South Park* raked it over the coals in a multi-episode slam, the cartoon equivalent of the dis raps that emerged during the East Coast/West Coast rap wars of the mid-1990s. I remember thinking about Tupac Shakur and Biggie Smalls as I slid my hand around Ivy's back and kissed her slowly, gently on the cheek, then her forehead, her eyes, brushed against her mouth, the space between our lips a mere atom.

Ivy allowed all of this to happen and in that final moment kissed me back, her eyes closed, her hands folded over her lap like a bridge-playing grandmother. The entire exchange, from the moment I brought up DLC to when Ivy finally relented and kissed me, lasted three minutes tops. Three minutes! What kind of world is this when the relationship between two civilized human beings can be irrevocably altered in the span of a radio pop song?

Ivy touched my face and pushed it away. She stared at her Mary Janes.

"Call me a cab."

"Ivy. That's crazy…"

"Call me a cab now please."

I went to my room and scanned the phone book for a cab company, but by the time I returned Ivy was gone. I ran out to the porch, palms sweaty, but there was no trace of her anywhere. I tried her phone but she'd turned it off. She must have ran, literally ran away from my touch and the prospect of additional fondling from the one and only Michael Bishop. I stood there awhile longer, my racing heart slowly returning to normal, panic subsiding to fatalism. I'd blown it, come on too strong, moved too quickly, and instead of having a full day with Ivy Chase to look forward to, now I had only this: loneliness. So I went back inside and set up my ancient Nintendo Entertainment System. I popped in *Mega Man 2*. It was the first video game I'd ever beaten, just two months after the car accident on Route 6. I used the Game Genie back then, a cheat device that provided the player with extra lives, health, ammo, you name it. Now, I played in absolute darkness, the compressed music of synthesizers and microchips returning me to my youth, to the 1980s, a world where I was the hero, where all bodily awareness evaporated and I could become beautiful, light, electric, where I could become the machine, the final resident of a post-human earth.

The Age of Anxiety, Fear & Indecision   (Part 2 of 3)

The Enigma of Keith Tedesco

I watched from behind a bush as the new kid slapped at Bobby McNamara's thick frame before taking a monster uppercut to the kisser. It was not an everyday sight for recess at St. Anthony's. Those nuns had us brainwashed—I watched the mass on television when my parents wouldn't take me, out of fear that God would strike our whole family down— and fighting was severely frowned upon not only by those frigid penguins who ruled us like the Black Riders of Tolkien, but also Jesus H. Christ Himself! Fighting equaled sin, and we all knew where sin would land you.

Damnation!

The Eternal Flames of Hell!

The children of St. Anthony's were grubby little monsters, ruddy at ten and eleven like the child miners I'd seen in Scrantonian history books. I half expected my peers to wear hard hats and carry tin pails filled with roast beef and liverwurst. My parents were not especially religious and had only sent me there because they were alumni, and gee, wouldn't it be nice to have a second generation St. Anthony's grad in the family? I learned to hide in the periphery of the playground—a lopsided parking lot craggy like the moon—hidden in a shallow trench of brush like a scientist observing an alien species, making occasional marks in my trusty red composition book. Clearly, the new kid had not yet learned the all-too-important lesson of how to make yourself invisible. He collapsed to the ground after the very first punch, even before a circle of jeering boys could form around them. I instinctively knew this boy was one of my own: narrow and snub-nosed, angel hair arms, slightly feminine mouth, Keith Tedesco. He didn't look like the others and I knew even then I should have made an attempt to save him, or at the very least go and inform one of the sisters about the brutality unfolding under their watch.

But I did not. I stayed put and thought about how strange it was to watch someone not named Michael Bishop suffer. How strange it was to gawk and do nothing to help. It was empowering, and that knowledge burrowed its way deep into my stomach and took refuge there, growing into something I would have to learn to contend with.

McNamara kicked Keith a few times. He cried and sniffled before finally one of those mysterious nuns swooped down upon them. The other boys scattered like struck marbles. The nun grabbed Keith by the ear and dragged him through the front doors of the church basement into the narrow hallway that served as our school.

I knew what would happen to him from experience. The nun would shove Keith into the boys' bathroom and leave him alone with his bruised ego to wash away his scrapes, to consider what impotency of the soul had brought him to such a miserable plateau at such a young age. I closed my notebook and snuck inside, my curiosity piqued. Michael Bishop suffering was not a new sight, but another boy, another human? This was practically the stuff of my beloved comic books.

The bathroom smelled like a hospital. The tiled floor alternated green and yellow. Keith gripped the sink with both hands. He'd stopped crying. He stared at his reflection in the mirror as though he was confused and riveted by what he found there.

I said hi. He said the same. We made no mention of the despicable beat down.

"What's in your notebook?" He finally let go of the sink and faced me.

I held it open for him to see. I'd spent the majority of my imprisonment in St. Anthony's doodling fabulous adventures starring Spider-Man and Luke Skywalker, the Apostles and Super Mario. I believed in fictional worlds and the Power of Christ with such intensity that I sometimes felt my heart swell with anguish for being a boy of the "real." I believed that God had spared me from the accident on Route 6 for a specific reason, that He had enveloped my fragile little body in an aura of white light because I was destined to do something great. That I would save people from themselves. A modern day superhero.

"You like comics?" he asked through a runny nose.

"I love comics."

"Who's your favorite character?"

"Spider-Man."

"I like MODOK, the Mental Organism Designed Only for Killing." He sniffed. "Do you want to come to my house after school and read my *Star Wars* comics?"

That's all it took to confirm my suspicions: Keith Tedesco was a kindred spirit. For the first time I connected with a contemporary, for the first time I knew what it felt like to not be utterly alone. From that point forward, I would have an ally with which to face the Scrantonian masses.

I didn't know then that Keith would soon become burdened with secrets. I didn't know then that I would fail him during his most desperate hour.

The Incident of Which We Do Not Speak

Back in college I used to drink a lot, often alone. On the Thursday before spring break, I ordered a pitcher of Yuengling by myself in a real hole in the wall, good old Gene's Place. Then I drank another. I drank until all those Big Important Undergraduate Thoughts And Feelings of mine tumbled out. I sat under dim lighting and hoped I looked mysterious, a golden person of superior worth.

I chose Gene's Place because it was one of the few places around the university not teeming with undergrads fixated on the Steelers, Panthers, Penguins or popped collars from Abercrombie. At Gene's Place I could be anonymous. And after twenty-one years of being Michael Bishop—lanky high school nerd turned lanky college hipster—anonymity was so very appealing.

But as alluring as solitude can initially seem, it's never as glamorous when you actually achieve it. I texted Oz. *CUM 2 GENES!!!1* But he didn't respond. I knew it was a long shot, that he had a seminar early the next morning. So I sat feeling bad about myself and listening to sad country songs while thirty-somethings lamented car payments. I figured the next best thing to Oz was Sloan. Oz and I had moved into an apartment after our freshman year, while Sloan became an RA in exchange for tuition remission. She still lived in Tower A with all those impressionable freshmen girls, and I wondered if she'd introduce me to a few of them. It took all my concentration to type a text message that didn't read drunk. *S. Miss you like crazy, grrl! Let's hang out. Can I swing by?* I ordered a shot of Crown and while signing the bill, my cell phone rumbled across the bar top. *Yes, friend. Come by.*

I left Gene's and walked through the undergraduate ghetto, the trash bag cluttered streets, sneakers dangling from telephone wires above. There was a crowd of underagers milling around outside one of the few dives they could get into. A couple made out in an adjacent alleyway, and I stood and watched. They were really going at it, this guy with a popped collar, his lady friend decked out in a too-short mini skirt, glitter everywhere. He groped her ass, pushed her against the wall, her hands tight on the back of his neck. I spat in the gutter—a vice I only indulged while straight thug boozing—and thought about my parents, how my mom had traded lousy job for lousy job ever since I was born, how my dad worked ten hours a day at his garage in sinking Scranton, how neither of them ever complained. Was this what they'd scrimped and saved for all those years? Was this the bright future they'd hoped for? Their son blowing their meager savings on liquor, drunk in a street, watching troglodytes dry hump? I dug out my iPod and put on some no name band from Omaha. I pretended that the couple stopped kissing the moment I passed.

Sloan met me in the Tower mailroom. I was sitting on

one of those uncomfortable gray couches they have in every dormitory in America. The elevator door dinged and there she was. Her pants were plaid and she wore a faded Steelers jersey, number 86 for Hines Ward. I remembered that not everyone stayed out all night searching for truth and solace in empty beer mugs and hoped she hadn't been sleeping.

"Friend."

"S."

Inside the elevator everything started to spin. I tried to hide how drunk I was by leaning against the wall and humming the tune to *Ducktales*. Sloan yawned and touched my shoulder.

"You're super hammered, aren't you?"

"This gentleman? Never."

She smiled. Her hair was wild and a little in her face. She looked best when she wasn't even trying. "I was going to watch a little *Twin Peaks* before bed. My sister sent me the DVDs. You up for that?"

The elevator doors opened. The hallway was completely dark and way too warm, everything smelling of burnt rubber, that familiar dorm odor I'd forgotten. Construction paper butterflies hung from the doors adorned with freshman names. *Jessica. Faith. Missy.* I wondered what I hoped to find here, what these women were supposed to offer me.

"I've never seen *Twin Peaks*," I said.

"Really? You'll like it."

Sloan had transformed her cold, cluttered dorm room into a livable space. She owned a potted plant and replaced it every time it died. As RA, she enjoyed a private bathroom and the space for an actual recliner, which Oz and I had lugged across Oakland from the Goodwill. She'd covered the white brick walls with magazine clippings and photos, all her favorite rock bands, posters of silent film divas. She sat on the bed, the covers a tangled ball at her feet, and fumbled around her nightstand for the remote, her computer tower an omnipresent hum.

"I always lose everything," she said.

"Mm."

She sprawled out on the center of the bed, and it was obvious I should take my place on the armchair. But I lingered by the doorway, playing with the buttons on my cardigan. Something about the notion of being in that chair frightened me. I wanted to be close to another human being. Right that second. I pushed up my glasses and sat on the far edge of the bed. Sloan didn't seem to notice, and when she turned back triumphant with the remote in hand she just smiled again, the loose collar of her jersey exposing her left shoulder, the long nape of her neck, the slight bulge of baby fat beneath her pert little chin.

"What?" she asked.

"Nothing."

She drew her knees close to her chest and scooted against the window that looked out over the stillness of late night traffic, the Cathedral of Learning—the 42-storied tower where we had classes—glowing in the distance like an alien spacecraft. "Do you want to sit closer?" she asked.

"Whatever."

We sat shoulder to shoulder against the wooden backboard. I remembered that dorm beds were so great for getting close to girls because of how narrow and long they were. They forced you to press against the other person, to really feel the warmth of their body. Sloan turned on *Twin Peaks*. She was halfway through the first season and I couldn't really follow it. It was like coming into a conversation midstream. So I sat and stared, fidgeted and thought. It took me fifteen minutes to realize Sloan wasn't paying attention either. She rubbed her palms against her knees and looked out the window.

"What do you think about yourself, Michael?"

"Excuse me?"

She shook her head, looked at me like I was the stupidest person in the vast expanse of time and space. "What do you think about yourself? We've been friends a long time and I'm curious."

I licked my lips. The room spun. "I guess," I started, "that I'm pretty much the biggest badass in the history of mankind. The Anti-Hitler if you will."

A couple on the floor above us was arguing and I wanted to stand up and bang on the ceiling. None of this was supposed to happen. I didn't do things like lie in bed with Sloan Smith well past midnight.

"I figured you were going to say something like that. Something sarcastic. You come off as clever and smart… and even pretty cute." She wouldn't look at me. "But I understand you. I know why you're always talking about how good looking you are and what a stud you are. Why you're always saying stuff that's so over the top that it's obvious you're being facetious."

I draped my arm over the headboard. Her hair brushed against my wrist. I didn't have a plan. "Enlighten me, S."

"You're completely insecure. You have no self esteem at all and I don't think you like yourself very much. You're terrified of intimacy," she said. "I just want you to know it doesn't have to be that way. You don't have to put on a show all the time, and definitely not for me."

I balled my fist and set it against my chin. "Do you realize," I slurred, "that everything on this entire planet baffles and terrifies me? Do you understand how insanely uncomfortable I am in my own skin? Do you get how often I fantasize about becoming someone else?"

She reached out and held my hand. "I understand, Michael. I understand you."

What I remember most about the entire drunken evening

is the not quite silent gasp I made when she leaned over and kissed me. Soon my right leg was draped over her left. Then we were prone, my hands on either side of her body. Her hair smelled like the clinical soap in Catholic school bathrooms. The computer buzzed, the fan wheezed.

Minutes passed before Sloan moved her face free from mine. She was on top of me, her arms propping her up. I knew she could feel my boner pressed against her leg.

"Are we sure we want to do this?" she asked.

I pulled her jersey over her head in response, my mouth on her right nipple, surprisingly small, something I wouldn't have expected, a stray black hair jutting out from the edge. Her skin tasted like salt water. Her body like the ocean. I cupped the soft flesh of her hips. The whole episode lasted maybe twenty minutes, and when it was over, we didn't say a word. We just lay there, staring at the ceiling, at the water stain overhead, listening to the quarrelling lovers above.

I woke to the hiss of infinite showers, the slap of flip flops against linoleum, the endless "I'm so fucking excited it's motherfucking Friday" convos. My head ached and my joints hurt and I wanted to slip out of bed and be by myself for ten thousand years in a cave in the Antarctic. But I never really liked the cold. Maybe Death Valley, some place in Nevada where the Army conducted all those nuclear tests. An atomic desert. Yes! That would be the perfect place for the type of boy who showed up drunk at one in the morning for a booty call with one of his dearest friends.

While sleeping, Sloan had looped her arms around my neck, her thumbs pressed against my shoulder blades. Her arms looked pale and fleshy in the morning sunlight and I wondered how a girl like that could lose her natural color overnight, her olive skin that really was beautiful. I squeezed the sheets and panicked. The acidic feeling in my throat told me I had ruined everything, that our friendship dynamic was irrevocably wrecked. I actually woke her with the phrase, "What up, dawg?"

She snaked her arms free, revealing her small breasts. The traffic was thick below us and a bus pulled up to the curb. Its robotic voice announced, "59U, the Waterfront."

"S?"

"Your breath smells bad."

"I know."

"Are you hung over? You want some water from the bathroom?"

Water? Water. It was wonderful to be once again presented with such a simple choice.

"I'm not sure." We stared at each other. "I should probably get dressed and going. Got a lot of stuff to do before spring break and all."

"Yeah, me too. I have a monster paper due in architecture. Going to be a complete shut in between now and break."

"Totally."

I climbed out of bed and tugged on my jeans and socks. Sloan yanked her jersey over her head. She slit her eyes at me, like she'd never really seen me before.

"Michael."

"Uh-huh?"

"Do you think maybe we should talk about... what happened?"

"Oh, yeah," I said. "Absolutely. Shoot."

She tilted her chin upwards, a movement I'd seen her do countless times in classes and during Important Discussions about issues like the nature of altruism in late-era capitalism and whether or not *Ghostbusters II* was as good a sequel as *Back to the Future II*.

"I think there's two choices here," she said. "What happened last night… it could really change our relationship at a fundamental level, and I think I'm ok with that, but before we go through with it, you're going to have to be one hundred percent sure that you're ok with it too. So either you go to your apartment, shower, get presentable and then call me up for coffee, or you don't. If you don't, we never mention this again. Everything goes back the way it was. Easy peasy."

My lips felt dry and I stalled for time by applying some chap stick and offering it to Sloan. "What do *you* want?" I asked.

"That depends on what *you* want."

"Ok. Well, I guess I'll go home and either call you or not call you."

She didn't miss a beat. "That's fine. That's the most preferable option I think."

"Most definitely. That's definitely the best outcome."

"Yes."

As agreed upon, I made the six block walk of shame to my shitty tenement. Oz had already left for his seminar so I stripped down to nothing and walked around the house, examining all my naked failings in the mirrors, my concave chest, my nonexistent ass, my expanding stomach and pink hue of cheek acne that would probably fester there well into my thirties. I turned on my computer and scanned Sloan's Facebook for clues.

Sloan Smith is craving a double latte from Kiva Han and a Turkey Devonshire from the Union Grill…

Clearly, she wasn't going to help, so I followed suit.

Michael Bishop is thinking about Ducktales. What a perfect cartoon for the Reagan-era! A millionaire duck swims in a tower filled with gold coins while his slave employees are worked to the bone!

I turned the shower as hot as it would go and scalded myself clean. I decided I wouldn't go to class that day. I felt a little pukey and figured the best way to atone for everything I'd done was spending the day at another crap bar and drinking myself miserable.

We didn't talk until after spring break, which I had spent in Scranton reminded of my friendless past. On my first night back in Pittsburgh, Oz told me we absolutely had to see some new movie opening at midnight, which we did, Sloan in tow in the backseat. We acted like nothing happened and fell into our predictable banter—"Did you hear the new Boy Least Likely album?" "Yeah, their old stuff is about fifty billion times better. Sell outs." We joked and jostled and that summer Sloan met Noah at a church picnic. We never spoke about what happened.

I'm still not sure what I should have done that night in college, if I should have swept Sloan Smith off her feet or never even slept with her to begin with. But what I'm absolutely convinced of is this: that our decision to brush that night under the rug and bury all our feelings directly contributed to what would soon befall all of us. The end of our friendships. The slow demise of affection. Like Keith Tedesco, the episode with Sloan lurked in the background, waiting, waiting, waiting to consume us all.

When It Dawned on Ivy Chase that I am the Greatest Man Who Ever Lived

Sunday afternoon, two days after what shall evermore be referred to as The Stolen Kiss Incident, I parked my car in front of the Dor-Stop, a breakfast joint in Dormont. Ivy had texted me asking to meet here, our first communication since she disappeared from my living room. I didn't like my chances. Breakfast is the least romantic meal of the day unless you've very recently shared a bed. It's harmless. It's what you do with your grandmother on her birthday. O breakfast! O lost!

To make matters worse, I'd spent the majority of my morning perusing the Facebook profile of one Tommy Mendocino, the aforementioned boyfriend of Ivy Chase. You can only look at someone's Facebook profile page if you're friends with them or if you're part of the same network, something academic like Harvard or location-centric like Scranton. And even though I did not live in New York City—the network that young Tommy subscribed to—it only took a few minutes to change over from Pittsburgh to NYC. And thus, the details of Tommy Mendocino's life were laid bare.

My greatest fears were confirmed. As Mendocino implied, Tommy was the prototypical Italian, thick and strapping in a polo from God knows where—some awful place like Abercrombie and Fitch—the buttons undone to the top of his meaty chest and gag-inducing chest hair, oversized medallion celebrating whatever patron saint he'd chosen at confirmation. He was olive-skinned with a five o' clock shadow. His hair was dark and filled with product. His body was lean, but muscular with hidden strength and false bravado from too many plates of baccala and cannolis and gnocchi drenched in meat sauce.

In short, Tommy was everything I'd felt insecure about since childhood. My father resembled this type of Italian and as a boy I desperately wanted to emulate him. Then my hair turned light and my skin grew to the complexion of a lit light bulb. In high school, I shot up to 6'1 while my weight stayed a ludicrous 135. Very little changed in the ensuing decade, and although I learned to overcompensate with wit and charm and hyperbole, the prototypical Italian still managed to make me feel small and impotent, like that little shit who went completely unnoticed throughout all those bloodsucking days at Bishop O'Hara.

The Dor-Stop was hot and cramped, tiny and full of windows. A sign above the cash register that said *God Answers Knee-Mail* made me want to punch somebody in the throat. I thought I'd outgrown Catholic rage in college, but I guess I'll always remain a petty man.

"Hi." The teen hostess was small-framed with too-big boobs, a rash of purple acne blooming on her forehead. I wanted to comfort her, to let her know that this too would pass, that she would not always be this painful looking girl who lived in Dormont, Pennsylvania smelling of grits and cheese. I gave her my name and asked for a table for two.

"You're Ivy's friend, huh?" She picked up a pencil and crossed a name off her list. "She's here. She told me to look for you. Dor-Stop's mostly regulars, hun."

The *huh* and *hun* made me want to leap across the countertop and kiss her. So full of folksy camaraderie! That would show Ivy Chase, hidden here among people who all knew each other's business. Look at me! The jovial Michael Bishop! The amiable, the fun loving, the oh so wonderful! I could infiltrate her world. I could become a regular at the Dor-Stop and be served my beloved feta omelet without even consulting a menu.

The hostess led me around a fern plant and there sat Ivy at a table barely big enough for two, her hair pulled back in a pony tail, her body concealed in an oversized Fordham sweatshirt. No makeup. I assumed this meant Ivy had dragged me to her home turf to break the bad news, that she loved her New Yorker carpenter and refused to leave him for a skinny nerd who subtitled *High School Musical 2* and displayed the first seven volumes of *Essential Spider-Man* on his bookshelf. Here in the Dor-Stop, she held the advantage. Here in the Dor-Stop, she could ensure that I wouldn't cause a scene.

"You two have fun, huh?" the hostess said.

I set my arm over the back of my chair and squinted. "This place better not suck."

"It doesn't. Best breakfast in Western, PA bar none. Get the waffles."

We studied one another. I'd worn a sports jacket over a 1989 memorial marathon t-shirt. I took off the jacket and puffed out my sad, little chest. "So. We missed the zoo. How'd you get home?"

"There's this really amazing thing. It's called the bus. It's totally awesome."

I nodded. I understood why someone would use humor to skate around the important issues.

"You didn't have to leave."

"I have a boyfriend."

"A long-distance boyfriend. Of two months."

"He's still my boyfriend."

Our waitress showed up. I glared at her and asked for waffles and coffee. Ivy said she wasn't hungry but would take a coffee too if it wasn't too much trouble. Unwillingness to break bread: another bad sign.

"I thought you said the food here was great?"

"It is. I'm just full. My dad always cooks a big meal before services."

"He's a pastor, right?"

"Wow. You remembered something."

"I remember everything you tell me."

"Ok then, Michael. Here's what I want to know. Why do you even like me? Is it random? Is there any specific reason? Is it easy? Convenient?" She smiled as she said all this. It was disarming, the way snakes must feel as they're charmed out of big wicker baskets.

"Why I like you? Isn't it obvious? You're a super awesome girl."

She sighed. She tapped her sneakers against the linoleum. My sinuses acted up and I very unattractively honked my nose into a napkin. I resisted the desire to open it up and have myself a look to make sure there wasn't any blood.

"Is that all you have to say?" she asked.

"Ok. Fine." I couldn't look her in the eyes. "I'm the type of guy who's stifled and frightened by pretty much everything. I'm half-expecting somebody to run up behind me at all times and punch me in the face. Because there has to be somebody out there, right? Somebody gunning for you? But when we're together I forget about that stuff. You make me... I don't know. Want to be happier I guess? More human?"

"Is that a question?"

"No." We locked eyes. "When we're together I'm better."

My food arrived and I ate in silence. The things left unsaid hung in the air like the smells of the griddle. I wanted to tell her how I always put women on pedestals and blamed this a bit on the Virgin Mary. I wanted to tell her that I liked her because she seemed so pure and uncomplicated, how she'd also been damaged at a young age, maybe fundamentally broken in some way. I wanted to tell her that I too had lost a friend and maybe, just maybe, we could save each other. But you never told girls that. This wasn't the time or place—spatially or historically—for grand, sweeping gestures. Hoping to be human was just the right amount of derring-do. And finally, apropos of nothing, Ivy looked up from her coffee and said, "I like you, Michael. You make me laugh, and it's obvious that underneath all the bravado you're actually a very good person. And I don't think I've ever been attracted to a guy like you before." She paused. "Don't make me regret this."

"I won't," I said. "I promise."

She let me pay, and when I suggested we drive to a park, she agreed. I held the car door open like an 18th century gentleman. On the way, I played "In the Aeroplane Over the Sea" by Neutral Milk Hotel in a blatant attempt to make it our song. We'd listened to it every car trip and Ivy sang along as we drove through the franchise heavy strip that led into the city. Her hand rested on the shifter and she allowed me to reach across that immeasurably vast space and envelop her milky white fingers between my own. I was winning. Unlike Super Mario, my princess did not wait in another castle.

I drove all the way to a park on the north side of the city, its gigantic manmade lake sloshing in the middle, petulant, as if it knew it didn't belong among trees and dirt and air and those luck fooled ducks. We found a secluded spot on the edge, parked, and walked hand-in-hand down a wooded trail to a bench that overlooked the slapdash shacks and glowing river beyond, the brute force of the mountains even further. We sat close. Our breath steamed. She nestled her head against my shoulder and I put my arm around her. Her stomach grumbled and I wished I'd convinced her to eat something. I kissed her and she kissed back. We drove to my apartment where I heard Oz in his room grunting and lifting free weights, an activity he engaged in every few months.

I worried Oz's presence would be an obstacle, but clearly it wasn't. Ivy shut my bedroom door behind her. I double-clicked on iTunes. I had a mix for these types of occasions inconspicuously titled *On the Male Orgasm and the Future of the Human Race* loaded with Belle & Sebastian and Pixies songs. Nothing embarrassing. Nothing too synthetic or rough. No Kanye. No Misfits. We didn't even take the quilt off the bed.

Ivy and I did not have sex. I was pretty sure she was not that type of girl. But she did remove her shirt and plain white bra. She was thick. Curvy. We made out and eventually she set me flat on my back, got down to her knees, and took me in her mouth with an expertise that made it clear she'd perfected her technique long ago. I lay there panting. Balling the covers with my fists. Delirious with joy. Ivy Chase. I should have known.

Election Night 2004

Two days before our country reelected George W. Bush, Oz experienced a holy revelation in the back of a Chipotle. He set down his fajita burrito, his eyes turned toward the heavens—or in this case, the fly trap covered ceiling—his voice taut and grave. It was nearing midnight and we were surrounded by the sweet drunk musings of our co-ed brethren.

"It's over," he announced after a dramatic pause. "Kerry's going to lose. He's going to lose!"

We stared at each other, red globs of hot sauce trickling down our pimply chins.

We mailed in our absentee ballots a month earlier, and now it was nearly upon us, November 2nd, the day we dreaded, the day we dreamed about. Oz had introduced me to Howard Zinn, Noam Chomsky, and I'd even secretly devoured the less cerebral works of Michael Moore, sat by myself through four showings of *Farenheit 9/11* just to shout "Kerry '04!" during the end credits in hopes that I could somehow make a difference in a nation of apathetic millions.

We attended the rallies, those nervous gatherings of students in sandals and vintage t-shirts, boys with patchy goatees and girls with hair down to their waists. We chanted his name, all the while glancing nervously from side to side, hoping this was all some elaborate joke, as if this monotone robot named Kerry was just a pretender, as if we were still waiting for a superhero of yore to swoop down and save us.

Oz and I had sacrificed friendships to the election. Had marched into the caf in Pitt Union and argued with former buds over abortion, gay marriage, the war, the war, the war. "Are you insane?" we asked. "Has the whole world gone fucking nuts?" An economics major we lived with freshman year told us he was voting for Bush because of 9/11. Oz gave him a black eye.

He had more on the line than anybody else. 293 Americans had died in the first Iraq conflict, Oz's father among them. With rumors of a draft looming, Oz was terrified of dying the same way. His father's helicopter had been shot down over Al Kut, and Oz often told us how his old man never accomplished his dream of working the land of his birth—upstate New York—and how differently Oz's life would have turned out had it not been for Desert Storm, how it had been his mother who pushed him into higher education, his mother who called him every other day and pleaded with him to be safe, safe, safe.

Most nights we descended onto Oakland and paced the streets, strung out on our own self-righteousness, drunk out of our minds, stoned on dime bags. We travelled the neighborhood in patterns—squares, triangles, figure eights—searching for vehicles with George Bush stickers. When we found them, we spat on their windshields. If we felt cagey we sliced their tires with blunt kitchen knives. Then we sloshed on over to Tower A and tried to meet freshmen women who cared about the wars in the Middle East, the fate of Israel, the declining supply of oil. Girls with ideals, girls with bangs, girls with glasses, girls who might take us into their dorm rooms and fuck us senseless for the collective good of the American left! And like so many of our sisters and brothers in arms, in those final days leading up to the election we succumbed to fear and self-defeat and tossed our hopes of a one-term George W. to ruin.

"We need to get out of Pittsburgh," Oz told me in Chipotle. "I don't want to be here around the Young Republicans, the hardcore Christians. I can't do it, Michael. How do you feel about a trip to my dad's place?"

In our first two years of college, Oz had often suggested we drive up to his father's cabin in the Adirondacks, but never before had we made the pilgrimage. He described it as a real man's man's place. A tiny cabin in the woods near a lake where we could fish and get drunk and stoned and be manly. His father had left the property to Oz's mother, and she couldn't bear to part with it, but neither could she step inside. Oz had free reign of the place and had even rigged up a generator for TV and video games back in high school.

"Should we invite Sloan?" I asked.

"Nah. Boys' weekend. I don't go camping with girls."

Unlike so many drunken plans—ideas of scaling the Cathedral of Learning with sweating bottles of Colt 45, schemes to build a functioning bra cannon like the one in the "Homer Goes to College" episode of *The Simpsons*—this one actually came to fruition. We woke up early the next morning—a crisp eleven forty-five—and loaded my Saturn outside the tenement with all the essentials: my Nintendo Entertainment System complete with *Ducktales*, the recent DVD rerelease of the *Star Wars* trilogy, a dozen or so of the final Spider-Man Clone Saga comics I was rereading for the tenth time, and of course, an outrageous amount of pot and beer.

Oz assured me he had fishing equipment at the cabin and that we'd catch so many trout that we wouldn't need food. I believed him, and shortly after noon we sped off toward the great unknown of the Adirondack Mountains, nine hours of *This American Life* queued up on my iPod. Road trip, ho!

We arrived late, exhausted, our bellies heavy with greasy drive through. An hour of dirt roads off of the highway plunging deeper and deeper into dead foliage, their branches bare in the November chill. The omnipresent hum of something organic, alien, maybe bugs, owls? I sure as hell didn't know. In Scranton, the closest we came to wilderness was the benign walking trails that hugged Lake Scranton and the occasional trip to the dam to drink and be merry. Oz's cabin sat atop a little hill that rolled down into a fishing pond— not a lake as Oz had claimed—no bigger than the swimming pool in Pitt's gym. The house was made of wood and had a porch that jutted out from the front door with two rocking chairs layered in dust and dead leaves. Oz moved aside a pile of bricks and produced a rust spotted key.

"Let's hit the hay," he said.

The inside was one big room complete with a bed and couch—where I'd be sleeping—and a green Sportman generator alongside a television and hot plate. I didn't know it then, but Oz's cabin was not that different from the lofts we would come to know in our post-collegiate lives, in our slow crawl toward an adulthood perennially pulling back the goal posts.

The next morning, Oz tossed a PBR onto my sleeping body and said, "Wakey wakey, eggs and bakey."

We drank and drank and drank. We smoked what for me was an unfathomable amount of pot. When it became clear that neither of us was in any state to go fishing, Oz and I divvied up what little remained of a bag of Twizzlers and savored them like a fine porterhouse. We hooked up the Nintendo and took turns playing *Ducktales*, beating the game again and again in ever quickening intervals. Its digital cakes and ice cream provided us little nourishment. We took turns reading my Spider-Man issues where Peter Parker watched his partner Ben Reilly—more a beloved brother than the genetically hatched clone he was—dissolve into dust after succumbing to clone degeneration following an attack by the Green Goblin. Many long-winded paragraphs of grief and regret from Peter about letting his best friend die followed. Oz didn't comment much on the issues, which was lucky, because there in the woods, drunk with my best friend of not even two years, I almost told him about the other best friend—Keith—and everything that had happened to him.

Instead, we watched *Return of the Jedi* on mute.

"You know this was supposed to be on the Wookiee planet originally?" Oz said, pointing to the Moon of Endor where Ewoks lived and loved and resisted the Empire's tyranny. "Wookiees instead of Ewoks. Can you imagine?"

"I know. And the Wookiee planet has a name, bub. It's Kashyyyk." I took a long drag from our last dying roach. "But I don't really mind the Ewoks."

"Me either." Oz grabbed the joint. "I like those tree houses they live in. It seems nice up there. All families and community. Living off the land. No worries but practical ones. I would like to live like that. I would really like to live like all those Ewoks."

We nodded in agreement. *Return of the Jedi* ended. There was Hayden Christensen superimposed onto our childhood memories, his douchebag smirk replacing the elderly Anakin Skywalker of old, yet another bamboozlement concocted by George Lucas, the man once responsible for so many of our dreams. Oz and I looked at each other, and finally, it could no longer be avoided. We had come to the great outdoors to shield ourselves from the election results, but I think we both knew even before loading up the Saturn that we'd eventually cave. There were no more pop culture distractions. We had reached the end.

"Do you want to listen to the results on my car radio?"

Oz stubbed out the little husk of a joint. "I've got a bad feeling about this."

We sat in the Saturn amid darkness and our final twelve pack of beer, the full moon reflected in the lake below us. First Georgia and Indiana and Kentucky turned red. Then West Virginia and Alabama, Oklahoma and Tennessee. Soon Bush marched straight down the country, from North Dakota to Texas. We were powerless to stop the Republicans and the anti-gay bastards from winning Idaho, Montana, Colorado, Florida, and finally, emphatically Ohio. There were no speeches. No grand declarations of victory. Bush's reelection would pass through the night like the Patriot Act, all shadows and secrets and speed.

I knew this was a moment I'd always remember, so I chucked an empty can of PBR out the window. It clinked against a nearby tree and ricocheted back against the front tire. I shuffled my Chuck Taylors, lyrics Sharpied on their sides. Here was the outcome we had dreaded for nearly a year, none more so than Oz who hadn't spoken a single word in over an hour. He held an empty can close to his face, slowly turning it, studying it like it was the most important object in the entire world.

"What do you think Sloan's doing right now?" he asked suddenly.

I watched him in the passenger seat. Of all the reactions from Oz I had imagined in the months leading up to the election—spazzing out and rioting across Oakland chief among them—this almost whispered question would not have cracked the top 1000.

"Sloan? I don't know." I remembered the previous spring, the night we'd drunkenly had sex. I could still see her nipple, that lone beautiful hair protruding from the edge. "Why?"

"Isn't it obvious?"

"Isn't what obvious?"

"I'm kind of in love with her. Not love I guess. She says I'm infatuated."

I stared at him. I understood from my high school experience that I was often oblivious to the emotional states of my friends. But this? To be confronted so directly with something I wouldn't have fathomed in a million years? I sat there stunned.

"She says you're infatuated? So you told her?"

"Last spring. I said I was in love with her and she said I wasn't. That we just spent a lot of time together and that I was confused. I try my best not to think about it now. Try to think of Sloan as just one of the guys, but it's hard, you know? When she goes on dates. When we're walking to class or wherever and the light catches her hair a certain way." He scratched at his beard. "It's hard."

"What's bringing this on all of a sudden? Why tell me now?"

"Just something I've been thinking about." He turned to face me. "Do you ever worry about finding someone?"

"Finding someone like falling in love finding someone?"

He nodded. "Yeah. I know we're really young, but I've always had this fear that I would never find anyone. Even when I was a kid and girls were supposed to have cooties and all that. Do you think it's even possible anymore? To really connect with someone?"

"Was the marijuana laced with something?"

"Seriously. Do you think we're ever going to find true love?"

I turned off the radio. I wanted to go back inside the cabin and sleep off my drunkenness and magically wake up in Pittsburgh to the familiar sounds of our hand-me-down coffee maker and the comp nerds downstairs prepping for their morning classes. I wanted to see busses whiz by and watch cute girls saunter across campus in their almost winter coats with books hugged close to their glorious chests. I wanted to be anywhere but the wilderness. I looked at Oz and considered his question. The truth was I had no idea.

Oz stepped out of the Saturn and started to strip. First his shirt, then his shoes and socks, then his pants and even his underwear. I watched him with the bemused expression of a drunk who's consumed so much alcohol that nothing seems odd. Oz stripping in the woods. Sure. Why not? But then he started to run downhill, and I mean really bolt. And even in my sorry state it was clear where he was headed. The pond below. The body of water I had scoffed at the night before.

"Oz!" I opened the door. "What are you doing?"

His legs pumped faster than I had ever seen—in fact, the closest thing to physical activity I'd ever witnessed Oz attempt was racing to the front of a car after someone else yelled "Shotgun!"—and he entered the water with a great big splash and a yelp that echoed through the moonlit darkness. I ran after him, stopping at the edge of the pond. He was kicking and struggling, and for a brief moment, I felt my throat clenching, the onset of panic. I counted backwards. It took a second to realize where he was headed: to the wooden platform floating near the opposite end of the pond, buoyed on the bottom by gray rubber that in the darkness appeared to be some kind of inner tube. He was only in the cold waters for maybe a minute, but standing there on the shore, it seemed to drag on endlessly.

Oz hooked an arm up over the platform, then a leg. He climbed up and sat on his haunches, tilted his wet face to the moon and howled a guttural cry, almost inhuman. I watched him for a long time, even after he stopped screaming, his heavy breathing slowly returning to normal. I watched him. I watched him and did nothing. Finally, when it became obvious he wasn't heading for shore anytime soon, I returned to my couch in the cabin and fell asleep to dreams of Oz's beloved Ewoks, their magical wilderness commune so high above us, so close to the perfect blue sky. In the morning, we pretended that nothing had happened and drove back to Pittsburgh in silence.

The Potluck Dinner of a Thousand Revelations!

It was flurrying when I picked up Oz outside the Cathedral of Learning. He stood alone on the sidewalk, a sleeping bag tucked under his arm. Ivy waved at him from the passenger side but Oz made no reply.

"Did you sleep in your cubicle?" I asked once he buckled himself in.

He touched his unruly beard. "I was grading student papers and reading some stuff for ludic pedagogy and kind of got onto this tangent on Twitter about the prosumer. You know, one thing led to another."

"The prosumer?"

"Are you kidding, dude? I've explained it 800 times. People used to consume media like television and books. Now they produce content for websites like Facebook and Twitter.

They generate the entertainment. The prosumer. We've been turned into workers 24/7."

"Oh, sure, the prosumer."

I had no idea what he was talking about, but what immediately became clear to me was that tonight we'd have to suffer through Oz the Sullen instead of Oz the Smart and Righteous Brochacho, the Hyde to his Jekyll.

"I got a C- on one of my papers," he whispered. "It was about all the things I care about. How the digital's this totally new thing because it's an open system. There's no denouement. And it has the power to liberate all the people of the world, to democratize information!"

I tried not to roll my eyes. I wanted to sympathize with Oz, and in many ways, I did. He was my friend, and I wanted him to be happy. But so often, he came off sounding like a lunatic. He needed to get away from the internet. He needed to turn off his iPhone.

"But these professors at Pitt," he went on, "they're too old school. Too hung up on the old texts, still clinging to old media. They're all apolitical cocks."

"A C- isn't that bad though," Ivy said.

"In grad school, an A- is a stern warning, anything in the B region is essentially an F. A C? That means it's going to be nearly impossible for me to nab a good committee, make the right connections, land a solid thesis advisor. C means community college. Everything is the worst right now."

If I'd learned anything from thousands of hours of sitcoms, now was the time when I should pull over, pat him on the back and deliver an upbeat pep talk to the applause of an approving and reverent audience. But Oz hadn't lost his job. No girl had broken up with him. The mother-in-law wasn't coming to visit. Oz's troubles were intangible, existential, metaphysical, a hundred other buzz words that meant close to the same thing: Oz was losing his grip on the everyday.

And to be quite honest, I didn't have any idea how to deal with that type of problem. I had bigger issues to deal with, namely our destination: Sloan and Noah's Potluck Dinner!

The Potluck Dinner was a significant ritual in the life of the modern twenty-something. We were far too old for keggers and could barely even recall those submerged, acne-laden desires that had driven us out of our tenements and into the frat parties of yore. The Potluck Dinner was the next step in our social evolutions, a dry run for the wine and cheese of adulthood. This potluck specifically was an excuse for Sloan and Noah to play house, to imagine what it would be like to be married, to have colleagues instead of friends, neighbors instead of drinking buddies. We all had to prove we were maturing at society's expected rate.

Because of this, choosing a dish to present at the potluck was a much more stressful proposition than one might imagine. I was not hauling burgers or grilled cheese. I'd made angel hair in asparagus cream sauce with a side of olive oil cheesy bread. The modern man needed to be able to cook, to make meal after dazzling meal for a rotating cast of bodacious bombshells. I had studied under Rachael Ray, Bobby Flay, Giada De Laurentis and everyone else on the Food Network, and could now whip up shrimp fra diavolo, chickpea curry, or spinach and artichoke stuffed portobellas, a stark contrast to my undergrad dark age when I lived off popcorn and pizza bagels, the sustenance of the nuclear era.

My Potluck recipes follow:

Angel Hair with Asparagus Cream Sauce

Ingredients:

   1 Box of Whole Wheat Angel Hair
   ¼ Stick of Butter
   A lot of asparagus
   3 cloves of garlic

Grated Parmesan Cheese
5 Cups of Nonfat Milk (Gots to be healthy, am I right?)

Cook 1 box of Angel Hair. Put a half stick of butter in a pot and let it melt down into goopy deliciousness. Add asparagus and garlic and stir continuously for five minutes to prevent burning. Then add 5 cups of the nonfat milk. Throw on grated cheese and stir until the mix starts to bubble, then set to simmer. While this is happening, take a knife and make a dozen or so cuts through the Angel Hair to make them into tinier pieces. Keep stirring. Then toss the macaroni in the pot and stir until all the liquid has been soaked up by the Angel Hair. Prepare to drop an H-Bomb on everybody's taste buds.

Olive Oil Cheesy Bread

Ingredients:

6 slices of fancy bread of your choice (What is fancy bread? Scholars debate over this daily.)
Olive Oil
Garlic Powder
Mozzarella
Feta

Set your six slices of patented fancy bread inside a toaster oven. Slather olive oil on the top and bottom of the slices. Then coat with garlic powder and mozzarella cheese. Finish off with crumbled Feta. Cook for five minutes on 250 degrees or until the cheese has melted. Prepare to be everyone's hero.

Ivy pried open the Tupperware and took a mighty whiff, obviously impressed by my culinary expertise. I had the defroster pumping and it was wonderful to watch the powdery flakes melt on the windshield, to squeeze Ivy's hand and see Oz fidgeting with his seatbelt in the rearview. Ivy turned around, smiled that famous half-grin of hers, and tried to give Oz a fraction of the solace she offered me. But in the gathering darkness, he looked pale, even more so than normal for a Pittsburgher in winter. Some people resembled their pets; Oz resembled his battered MacBook.

Ivy patted his hand. "One of my friends from my father's church is coming. She's really smart and totally gorgeous. Maybe you'll hit it off."

"Yeah, maybe," Oz muttered.

She nodded. We didn't speak for the rest of the ride.

Sloan and Noah lived on the second floor of the Rummage House, a complex of subsidized lofts intended for working artists. My friends only qualified on account of some nonsense Sloan cooked up during the rental interview about a 600 page critique of amateur Enlightenment era art she was writing, a project so dry sounding that the owners—two Woodstock hippies, now married and fat with industry —would never actually request to see it, let alone read it. Originally an art deco car dealership, the Rummage House was converted into an apartment building two decades earlier, complete with curving staircases and huge rectangular windows that overlooked the brick and mortar of Shadyside. From outside, it looked like a decrepit warehouse and many of the yuppie gentrifiers called it an eyesore and made regular complaints to the city council, or so Sloan liked to claim. I didn't care much either way. I liked it simply because I'd always envisioned myself as the type of person who would one day have friends who lived in lofts, high above the petty squabbles of the hacking individuals I'd grown up with in Scranton. I liked to visit the Rummage House and gaze out into the heart of the city and feel superior to everyone I went to high school with who'd remained behind in eternally bankrupt Scranton, a flat nexus birthed over an ocean of ruined mines.

We arrived fashionably late. Sloan and Noah greeted us with glasses of red wine. Unremarkable alt folk strummed over the computer speakers. Their apartment was one enormous space, as big as my place minus the walls. The floors were hardwood and Sloan used a long bookshelf and an Ikea couch to give off the impression of rooms and division, defeating the purpose of a loft in my opinion. Noah's sports memorabilia and Playstation 2 sat in a cardboard box in the back of the closet. Sloan had drawn question marks on the box in bright purple marker, the headstone of Noah's bachelorhood.

After the initial pleasantries, Sloan returned to the small crowd gathered around her computer. I recognized a few people, mostly hipster baristas from Arefa's and a few of our undergrad acquaintances. Notably absent was anyone from Digital Deluxe. Maybe because of Junie?

"Get in the picture, guys. Get in the picture." Sloan snaked through the crowd and adjusted the webcam above her computer.

I hung back with Noah. I'd never seen her do her counting project up close. Ivy and I had discussed Sloan's peculiar habit and she thought it was "interesting but strange." Ivy admitted she wished Sloan, someone she'd known since childhood, would channel her energies into something a little more positive. And Oz? He resented the counting solely on the fact that Sloan had 8,000 followers while his Twitter feed—comprised mostly of unintelligible rants about his studies—languished in the low dozens. Couldn't she be more political, Oz had asked me in private?

"Count with me," Sloan said to the group. "217,417. 217,418. 217,419."

She spoke quickly, and soon, our fellow partiers matched her speed and intonation. When they reached 217,438, Sloan reached up and turned off the webcam. A few of the onlookers clapped. Most did nothing. One looked away and caught my gaze from across the room. It took me a second to put two and two together, to reconcile my previous existence—that sadly religious and dumbfounded boy who had attended Bishop O'Hara in discounted suits and ties—to this world of lofts and cities and Twitter. Before me stood Elaine Tedesco, returned to me from the ether of our shared and traumatic past, the sister of my dead best friend Keith.

Elaine didn't dress like the others. No jangly, '80s earrings. No swooping bangs or outrageous patterns hunted down in the wilds of Goodwill. Elaine wore blue jeans. Elaine wore the most average cardigan in the glorious history of cardigans. And she was still beautiful! Dark hair that fell to the small of her back. That slightly upturned nose that gave off the impression of a woodland sprite, a Princess Zelda even! This was the girl who had powered my masturbation fantasies during those most reverent years of self-abuse! This was the grown-up version of the girl who had utterly captivated my pubescent mind with her portrayal of Emily Webb in the school production of *Our Town*. This was the woman who didn't know the truth about her brother's death, how I had failed him in his final days.

This was Elaine Tedesco. In Pittsburgh.

She strode past the dinner table and gave me a shocked smile, a quick tilt of her head that caused a loose strand of hair to fall across her right eye. Ivy came up behind her and gingerly touched Elaine on the shoulder. "Michael, this is my friend from church I was telling you and Oz about."

"We've met," I said.

She waited for an explanation, but I was completely ill-equipped to describe the burden of loss that connected us.

"We went to the same high school," Elaine said. "Michael was best friends with my little brother."

I raised my fist to my mouth and bit at the loose skin around my knuckles. I'd never told anyone, not Oz or Sloan or Ivy or Noah, about Keith, and I sure as hell didn't want it coming up at a potluck dinner. I hadn't even cried at his funeral! I couldn't even remember the last time I cried!

"I bet Michael was cute in high school," Ivy said.

Elaine reached up and patted my head. "He was such a little nerd."

"Ha ha ha!" I said much too loudly, my eyes bugging out like some sort of worried anime character. "Ha ha ha!"

I was saved when Sloan produced trays upon trays of appetizers: so many shapes and sizes of crackers! So much hummus! So much cheese! We stood around the food and grazed like cows only occasionally stopping to mention The Election or Obama or Arcade Fire. Not that I could really focus. I couldn't take my eyes off Elaine.

"Elaine." My voice cracked. A few people chatting about the political overtones of the recent death of Captain America turned to look. "How... How long have you been in Pittsburgh?"

"Six months." She bit off half of a gorgonzola covered cracker and held the remainder in her dainty hand. "I met Ivy at her father's church, and she was nice enough to offer to show me around."

"Wow! That is really, really awesome and potentially the greatest thing I have ever heard in my young life," I said. "What are you doing in town?"

"I'm an Epidemiologist. At UPMC?"

A man in a gray vest and ironic Snoopy t-shirt rubbed his soul patch. "What's that mean exactly?"

"I'm studying how cancer spreads across the population. I basically research virus outbreak and how something can overtake a demographic."

I blinked at her. We did not have jobs that involved "research" or "viruses" or "demographics." We churned coffee beans. We taught freshmen about Paulo Freire's *Pedagogy of the Oppressed.* We scanned the dubious script of *Kangaroo Jack* for typos and inconsistencies. What a strange creature here among us.

Elaine Tedesco!

She reached out and touched my elbow, *my* elbow! I was half-afraid that the sum result of all those masturbation fantasies would explode my penis and splatter all over her tasteful pants.

"Michael," she said very seriously, "if you have time, I'd like to go out for coffee and catch up."

I pawed at the pyramid of crackers and shoveled a handful into my mouth. I raised a finger to indicate that I would respond just as soon as I'd finished chewing and could speak without embarrassment. Coffee! What earth-shattering development was next?

I swallowed hard. "Coffee is fine."

"I love Ivy, by the way," she said. "This isn't a meeting of the romantic variety if that's what you're thinking, you big goof."

"Oh no! I would never even entertain that possibility." I showed my teeth. And before I could utter anything else unbearably stupid, Sloan emerged from behind the kitchen island and announced that dinner was ready, that I had survived the first portion of this horrific evening and could move onto the Meal of My Discontent.

⁂

We feasted on Sloan's spinach mushroom quiche and Noah's sad attempt at Caesar salad. We ate baked vegan macaroni and cheese and a sushi boat one of Sloan's co-workers had picked up from Sushi Boat. Noah looked up from my angel hair dish and announced, "Of course you'd make this Dago food." And Ivy—oh Ivy!—she possessed a confidence and grace unheard of in a twenty-two year old girl! She retold us the plot of an experimental play she'd seen, something fresh during her trip abroad to Spain, an existential comedy about a rabbi and priest trapped in a burning plane hurtling down somewhere over the equator.

"Oh, I barely even believed it," she said. "Down some little narrow alley in a garage. That's what it's like there. People are just putting on plays for no reason. It's just so much more real there."

We'd all felt that way at some point, if not overwhelmingly so during our own college heydays, and that warm remembrance made us watch Ivy with an equal mix of nostalgia and heartbreak. Soon she'd enter the real world. Soon she'd leave college and those funny little ideas of hers behind. Soon she'd earn her pay like the rest of us, the walking dead, the overeducated and directionless. I cleaned my plate and watched Elaine two seats away from me looking as radiant as ever. I tried not to be consumed.

When everyone finished eating we began in earnest with the wine and the rum, the Pabst and the whiskey. I thought we'd embark on that familiar adventure of dissecting pop culture minutiae and making ourselves important until the proverbial cows came home. I thought this would be another agreeable evening but one I'd fondly forget in a few days, another chapter in my Mid-Twenties, an e-book that was starting to run together, the only discernable change in page after page the rising and falling of temperatures, the earth swinging closer or further from the sun. On all accounts, I was wrong.

"Listen," Sloan said. She chimed her fork against her empty wine glass. It was a self-conscious gesture. We could tell from the way she arched her eyebrows, how her mouth turned into a smirk. As if tapping one's wine glass was an act reserved for Adults. "We don't want this to be a big announcement or some crazy production or anything like that so we've decided just to tell you." She took Noah's hand. I wondered if they were getting a dog, maybe something small and house bred Sloan could carry in her purse. Maybe they'd let me name it Uncle Jesse the Dog or Osama Bin Doggen. "Noah and I are engaged."

A few people clapped. Some held up drinks in toast. Ivy squealed with joy and rushed over to lock Sloan in a bear hug. They embraced. They made strange noises I thought were only uttered during sorority pillow fights. I caught Noah's gaze but he just waggled his eyebrows like a game show host and shrugged, Junie Censulla a memory as remote and unthreatening as our goopy primordial pasts.

And me? What did I think about the whole arrangement? I really couldn't pinpoint my feelings. I'd watched these two come together, grow serious, move in. I'd even listened to Noah discuss the engagement ring. But for some reason none of that ever seemed real. They weren't a legitimate couple. They were like actors in a rom com. Sure, they look the part, but the whole time the audience knows it's a lark. Even though I loved Noah, I think subconsciously—I know, I know, I'll never use that word again—I always believed that Sloan would come back on the market, that Oz and I would be single, that things would return to how they were in college, our most natural equilibrium.

"You're getting engaged?" Oz crumpled his napkin. The disdain in his voice was palpable and everyone turned to look. The room turned silent.

"That's what they said, Oz. Why don't you congratulate the happy couple?"

I patted him on the back and smiled wide, tried to turn his sarcasm into a corny little moment we could talk about at the wedding, the baby shower, the first Holy Communion, the rest of their lives. I remembered his long ago revelation in the woods, that at one time he believed that he'd fallen in love with Sloan Smith. But that was years ago. Nearly a full election cycle! I wondered whether or not he still harbored feelings for Sloan, and what he would have thought if he knew I'd slept with her in a moment of characteristic weakness. Oz. How could I be friends with someone for so long and still understand so little about them?

Oz nodded vaguely in their direction, excused himself, and hid in the bathroom. His pained reaction set my Spider-Sense tingling, but I just wasn't sure how I could save him. I stared at that bathroom door all too aware of Elaine Tedesco's presence. I remembered what happened to her brother.

Noah—always the product of the ra-ra can-do attitude of the sports world—refused to allow Oz's reaction to dampen the occasion. Sloan was prone to sulking whenever some personally meaningful act didn't go exactly as planned, and wary of her storming off to the bedroom as we'd seen time and again, he grabbed her by the elbow and steered her toward the kitchen cupboards.

"Let's celebrate," he said. "I picked up a couple bottles of champagne. Let's drink them and head to the Cage."

"Hear motherfucking hear," I added.

We drank. We laughed. We danced to 1980s synth pop. Sloan and Ivy held hands and twirled to the music like the childhood friends they must have once been. After a few songs Oz returned from the bathroom, his cheeks a little pinker, his disposition somewhat promising. He smiled like the Oz we remembered, the one from my birthday, the one from college, the jovial and good-natured. He accepted a glass from Elaine and just like that the whole event was swept under the rug, a hilarious non-sequitur in the otherwise tightly plotted black comedy of our lives.

So we stumbled outside and crammed into vehicles. Ivy sat up with me, and Sloan sat in back between Oz and Noah who discussed how much snow they thought we'd get—it had already accumulated like cotton candy at our feet, turning thick and wet during the potluck. The entire city of Pittsburgh stays home during snowfall and we rocketed through those abandoned streets like a spaceship, pressing together for warmth, Kanye blasting on the radio as we screamed along, our breath fogging the windows with tangible proof of our joy. I took Ivy's hand and gently kissed her knuckles. In moments like this, I still believed that anything was possible, that I was special and unique, that an untold treasure trove of glory and never-ending happiness awaited me in the not-too-distant future. I closed my eyes and imagined the entire world ablaze.

Of course, as all true alcohol enthusiasts know, our euphoria did not last. Champagne gives a special kind of buzz, or maybe, for people like myself who rarely drink it, champagne makes you feel that this night will be out of the ordinary, that this night will become something truly memorable. It doesn't mix well with cheap pitchers of keg kicked Yuengling. It doesn't mix well with the second floor of the Squirrel Cage.

Within an hour, all of the guests outside of our normal circle left. Goodbye, Snoopy shirt! Goodbye, Elaine Tedesco! They left us to our familiar places on the second floor, the champagne buzz dead and buried, to listen to Noah talk about the failures and successes of his YMCA biddy basketball team. No one responded, so he proceeded to eviscerate the time travel logic in *Back to the Future*.

"Just hear me out," he said. "The earth rotates around the sun right? And it's moving at what? A thousand miles per hour? So if Marty time travels and the Delorean always brings him to the same exact spot he left from, shouldn't he be thousands of miles away from the earth? Somewhere in space? That'd be an awesome movie. The Libyans show up, they see some serious shit when McFly hits 88, then he suffocates in cold outer space."

I forced a chuckle. Ivy and Sloan just stared at the television. We sat there drinking and feeling terribly old yet immature, and then, out of nowhere, Oz climbed down the narrow stairs and walked straight through the exit. He did not say goodbye. He did not leave money for the check. His half empty glass stood sweating on the wooden table.

"Well," Noah said. "Maybe we should call it a night."

By the time I dropped Noah and Sloan off, the roads and sidewalks and trees and power lines were completely covered in snow, nearly four inches' worth. Everything hummed with the stillness of a snowy urban night when everyone's gone indoors, when the whole world seems to have opted for golden silence. We were driving through Squirrel Hill on the way to the highway when Ivy moved her head to the crook of my shoulder. I wanted to slip down into the music of her body, into her blood, and see how each and every part of her functioned, how flesh and water in combination made Ivy Chase whole.

"I'll call my dad," she whispered. "He knows the weather's bad. I'll say I'm staying over at Sloan's. He remembers her from when I was a kid."

I didn't need to be asked twice. I returned to my house and led Ivy inside by the hand. Oz's room was next to mine. His lights were off. I figured he'd returned to the Cathedral of Learning to moan about how backwards university English departments are and their refusal to acknowledge the digital as a legit field of study, but to be on the safe side, I played *Ghostbusters II* loud in my room. I never was sure if putting on a movie was preferable to Oz over the sounds of sex, but I'd certainly rather listen to Bill Murray over Oz grunting and panting like a buffoon atop of some strumpet.

Ivy and I made love next to the radiator under my Ninja Turtles blanket—the bed was too cold—and when Ivy pushed me onto my back and got on top, I watched the Ghostbusters use an NES Advantage to pilot the Statue of Liberty through New York where somewhere that baby carpenter Tommy

Mendocino lay waiting to ambush our hero: moi. I came as the Ghostbusters defeated the nefarious Vigo. This was Love in the 21st Century.

Scientists have long known that when men ejaculate their brains shut down for approximately two seconds. With Ivy Chase, this was not the case. With Ivy Chase, time slowed down—or at least my perception of it—and the billions of neurons linked to thousands of synaptic connectors inside my anxious, little head went absolutely loco. My wormlike hippocampus gland shuddered against my medial temporal lobe and these vibrations birthed an alien fantasy world I lost myself in for what felt like hours, days, months, even if only two ejaculatory seconds passed in the real world.

We are on Mars, but we are no longer young. This is not the place for youth. It is where the elderly are shuttled off to, the assisted living ranches of outer space. We sit on Mars under big glass domes and tilt our wrinkly heads toward the sky. They have us lined up on an infinitely long porch, our bodies connected to hundreds of computers, impossible machines that shout "Beep!" and "Yip!" complete with nugget dials and sensors that make us nervous. We cannot move. The machines are too big, unruly, all hooked in intravenously through our mouths, noses, ears, belly buttons, anuses, genitals.

We sway back and forth on the rocking chairs of our destruction.

Some of us listen to music. We avoid the old crooners, the Frank Sinatras and Dean Martins and Sammy Davis Juniors and Peter Lawfords and Joey Bishops or anyone else associated with the Rat Pack. We prefer gangster rap. We sit on our death rockers and tentatively nod to "Juicy" by Notorious B.I.G. and "California Love" by Tupac Shakur. We have forgotten which one of these urban youths died first, but either way it's a tragic shame perfectly suited for a group of people whose hormones first went ape shit during the 9/11 attacks.

We are shocked at how old we have become. Liver spots! When we saw our grandparents' hands as children it seemed like a sick joke. Saggy skin. Pale complexions. Baldness. We look like babies! And maybe that's all aging is. The universe was born and then it expanded. After a period of time it began to rapidly compress. Maybe the aging process is the contraction of the human spirit.

No one talks much anymore, but we do have Facebook on our machines. So we can make wall posts from time to time. We rarely do however. What is there to say really? Hi. I'm still on that porch on Mars. What up? So we sit and watch the dead sky and wait to die. Sometimes we play Nintendo games. Very few of us can even make it past 4-1 on Super Mario Brothers these days. The digital apparitions of our youth torment us so.

Because the sky burned out so long ago, we no longer have Earthian conceptions of time. But He comes at what was once referred to as midnight. It begins as a speck in the distance, a reminder of our former planet. But the speck grows larger. Fast. Fast. Fast. Within seconds He is above the dome with His arms extended. He sits in a diamond encrusted chariot pulled by six stainless steel horses. They breathe fire.

It is Kanye.

He beams down Star Trek-style and folds his arms over his muscular chest. His glasses reflect the black hole sun. He has not aged a day. He is the same old Kanye we remember from our youth, hands outstretched to the heavens in a diamond shape. We want to shout and scream. We want to bask in the glory of this miracle, that Kanye West has returned from His adventure across the cosmos to learn how to cheat death, to end and potentially reverse the natural flow of time.

Kanye West has come to save us from ourselves.

Yet we are troubled. Why hasn't He spoken? Why won't He speak? We remember how He disappeared in the early 21st *century, how He left in an Escalade rocket claiming He would only return when He'd discovered the meaning of life. Why are His hands above his head? Why won't He speak?*

We lean forward in our rocking chairs. Our machines gasp in agony. Our bodies have not experienced this much stress in centuries.

Kanye opens His mouth. He booms.

"The Kanye cometh! Ye have bequeathed your spiritual birthrights. I have naught come hither to save you. I have travelled the stars and have returned to tell you this: Ye have failed. The dearth of your anonymity astonishes. No one knows you. The world is not aware of your names. Thou art one in a crowd of billions. Because of that, thou doth not matter, thou doth not exist."

Electricity cackles between His open hands. Then a solid yellow light. An explosion that blows everything back for miles, the endless porch decimated, the machines caved in, the rocking chairs shattered. Bodies everywhere. The dome explodes. We are blown into the emptiness of Martian space. Kanye returns to His chariot and rides toward the burning black tentacles of the zombie sun.

🌉

Finally, my hippocampus steadied, and I found myself alongside my bed with Ivy Chase on top of me, my penis still inside her. She whispered that she could feel my heartbeat through my fading erection, and this bout of hyper intimacy made me sweat. Only two seconds had passed. No more. She leaned forward and kissed my moist shoulder. She wrapped her arms around my narrow back while I closed my eyes, fighting conflicting images of love and death, Mars and Kanye.

We cuddled afterwards which always made me nervous. Spooning is the true signifier of whether or not you're in a relationship. You don't cuddle one-night stands. You don't spoon friends with benefits. And nothing is more embarrassing than when one person puts their all into cuddling and the other person just lies there stiff as an indignant corpse. So thank God that Ivy allowed me to nuzzle up beside her, to wrap my arms around the slight swell of her stomach and caress her moony breasts. She tickled my legs, ran her fingers through my hair. And in this silence we were happy.

"I broke up with Tommy," she whispered.

I didn't reply. I assumed she'd taken care of that messy business earlier, maybe even on the day of our Dor-Stop rendezvous. I hadn't thought out the mechanics. I hadn't thought out the very human toll our coupling would enact.

"Did you tell him about me?"

"No. I think that'd hurt him too much. He'll find out through Facebook in a little while."

She rolled onto her back and took my hand between hers, held it close to her heart so I could feel its steady drumbeat. "I told my dad about it and he was kind of disappointed."

"What? Why?"

"He met Tommy a couple of times. Liked him. Tommy is a really big Christian."

Her father, the pastor. I'd almost forgotten about him. Religion was so ironic that I didn't always remember that some people took it very seriously, that some people didn't see the inherent hilarity in that lovable scamp Jesus Christ. I tried to look spiritual. I assumed this meant furrowing my brow.

"I went to Catholic school for thirteen years," I managed.

"He wants to meet you." She rubbed at my cheeks. "I want you to meet him too. We're a very close family. We even do community service together."

Surely this was reason to panic. "I'd love to meet him."

"Great." She kissed me gently on the lips. "Come over for dinner some day after work. He'll totally love you."

It was almost four in the morning now and I could hear

someone, somewhere shoveling the snow from their driveway. The music of scoop, toss; scoop, toss. This was our lullaby and we fell asleep in each other's arms, our bodies huddled for warmth, the odor of sex clinging to everything, the whole room smelling of sweat and latex and the plastic of too many products.

On the Defining Moment of Our Generation

Every generation has a moment that so perfectly crystallizes their time and place that it's looked back on as the watershed event, the precise second when that era's youth stood proud and united and free. Go back to the birth of this country. 1776. The signing of the Declaration of Independence. Sure, the founding fathers weren't really clear on that whole "right to bear arms" thing but other than that, their ideas were pretty solid—the big S notwithstanding. That was a defining moment. Nearly a century later and Lincoln was stabbing Southerners in the face with American flags. Another defining moment. How about World War II? VE-Day to be precise. A wave of euphoria before all those concentration camp pics came back, before we dirtied our hands with that manmade love poem affectionately referred to as the atom bomb. That was a defining moment. And the 1960s? Who could forget them? A generation every teen afterwards has been bluntly informed they can never live up to. They were so awesome they got two moments: the 1968 Democratic Convention or Woodstock. Take your pick. Either you're an optimist or a pessimist. Oh yeah, and remember that little blip on the radar occasionally referred to as Generation X? That feeble group of slackers who paved the way for our slide into obscurity and utter inconsequence? You could go with the Reagan Revolution, Live Aid, the Collapse of the Berlin Wall, the Challenger Explosion, Tiananmen Square, the Oklahoma City Bombing, or even the OJ Trial, but for my money Kurt Cobain's death is where it's at. At least they had a grimy grunge rocker to splatter his brains out over a cabin wall. At least they had Saint Kurt to shout a great big "Fuck You" to civilized America.

So here we are. Generation Y? The Millennials? Digital Natives? Branding's handled by the historians. It may surprise you to learn that our moment has already passed, that our defining moment didn't happen all at once but spread virally, something characteristic of our very natures. It's not 9/11. No, in the history books of the future—books that will only exist in the zeroes and ones of the digital—9/11 will never be able to compete with the true dawn of 21st century narcissism.

Facebook.

Social media is the shared experience of the 21st century.

I was still in college when it happened and didn't understand it at first. In high school, I'd created account after account on various message boards—mostly for video games or emo music—and had written four years' worth of angsty entries in internet journals—this was before the term "blog" permeated our collective consciousness. What was so great about having a random picture of yourself on the internet?

Everything.

Within a week of signing up I had three hundred friends,

pals from Pitt, goons from Bishop O' Hara, the grand accumulation of my lifetime's acquaintances. First came the profile pictures. That tiny box, a smattering of pixels amounting to a smile cocked just so, the body in stasis, the light frozen for all eternity. People started bringing cameras everywhere. To parties. To the bar. *Take our picture for Facebook*, they'd say. *I can't wait to see this on a Facebook album.* Suddenly we were taking pictures with the express intent of posting them on the internet, to prove our individual self-worth!

Because that's what Facebook does. It makes everyone matter. It gives everyone a voice, albeit a voice contained within the parameters of the Facebook corporate entity. Facebook is reality television for the everyday human. It makes a spectacle out of everyone. It dispenses fame and importance to a society obsessed.

During the early days of my courtship with Ivy Chase, I was uploading pictures from high school and came across one of me and Keith Tedesco leaning against the hood of his freshly washed Honda Prelude, its candy apple paint job shimmering in the coal dust Scrantonian sun. There we were. So young. Our faces happy and full of promise, tipped to the sky as though waiting for something too wonderful for language to happen.

But Keith died before Facebook. He missed out on everything. So I sat there at my computer as I'm prone to do and wondered whether or not he would have approved, if he would've wanted to live on in the digital ether for all time. Because according to Facebook's Terms of Service, when you upload a photo you surrender all rights to the Facebook Corporation. They save pictures on their databases, servers as vast and powerful as any nuclear submarine. They own those pictures and can do with them what they please. So if I uploaded Keith Tedesco into the mainframe I could potentially see his grinning mug fifty years down the road on the side of a bus promoting the Facebook E-Reader or Facebook

Alternative Fuel or Facebook Moonbase. In this small way I could make him live forever.

There really wasn't much of a choice.

I uploaded my long dead friend and turned him loose onto the chaos and speed of the internet. I tagged him in the photo and stared at his face. Can people have a digital afterlife? Can humans exist beyond death in the cold womb of the machine? Are we that far away from digital graveyards? I pressed my face to the screen, my eyes burning, and tried to make out the individual beams of light that made up Keith's face. I wanted to hold the internet in my hands. I wanted to shake it and beat it and bathe in it and demand that it protect me from the only thing that truly mattered, the only thing anyone with even a shred of common decency and sense had ever really feared.

Death.

Death.

Death.

The Age of Anxiety, Fear & Indecision (Part 3 of 3)

This Is How the Century Is Born

When you are sixteen Keith Tedesco purchases a Honda Prelude. Your heart swells with joy and jealousy eternal, but Keith is your best friend, your only friend, and therefore you will be able to ride in it whenever you want. The Prelude is not boxy like your mother's station wagon. The paint is not rusted like your father's pickup. Its engine hums with the faint, mysterious language of sex. Keith loves the car so much he often sleeps in it. He parks in his parents' garage, and at night, when he is sure his family is asleep, sneaks downstairs in his boxer shorts and dozes off in the backseat. Sometimes he signs onto Instant Messenger before bed and the two of you yak for hours about how much you hate everyone at

Bishop O'Hara. His screen name is PreludeMan84. Yours is MikesScreename. Neither of you can fully imagine a world outside of Scranton, but you tentatively discuss The Future. Maybe you will get into the same college. Maybe you will be roommates. These thoughts comfort you. But Keith says he hopes he never gets old. He'd rather be dead.

You have gone to Catholic school your entire life. You do not take the Lord's name in vain. You do not believe in Abortions. You hate Homosexuals. You are certain that this world is a trial to get into Heaven. You light candles alongside the old Italian mamas for your soul and especially for Keith's. In the crucible of St. Anthony's he shed his nerdy origins and turned maverick. He is the first to try a cigarette, the first to sneak into an R-rated movie, the first to break curfew. He is dangerous. He is serious. And the girls are drawn to him for the same reasons the other boys dislike him—he is mature and grave. He has a super cute girlfriend named Annie. He has an older sister named Elaine who dazzles you with her performance as Dolly in the high school musical. You whack off to Elaine's picture in the yearbook, her loopy cursive with those heart dotted i's proclaiming: *Stay cool as an ice cube, hun!!!! xxxxooooxxxoooo* This greeting is enough to get you started. And because you and Keith are so close the other boys occasionally call you "faggots." You weren't aware you had this much rage inside of you, but there it is, pulsating and so very alive.

On the shortest day of the year, you and Keith hit a hundred miles per hour on the snow-covered Route 6. Fear. Fear. Fear!

This is how the century is born.

FEBRUARY

In the cafeteria you tell Keith about "emo." You discovered it during long hours trolling the internet for anything to make you feel connected, to make you feel part of a whole. Neither of you are completely sure what "emo" is, but you know it somehow involves alt rock band Weezer. In its members you see powerful premonitions of what you can become: still skinny, still pale, still nerdy, but confident. Confident with girls. Weezer sings about Nightcrawler and Kitty Pryde, two of your favorite X-Men. Weezer sings about heartbreak, loss and rejection. You do not understand that being called "emo" is an insult. You do not yet see the value in irony or apathy. This is all to come. Within a few years you will look back on this moment of your life and cringe. You will refer to this period of time as your "well intentioned, but gravely misinformed earnest years."

While driving up and down Route 6, while listening to Weezer at full blast, Keith tells you that he has come to an important decision. He has decided that he is going to think about possibly having sex with Annie. You tell him "Ballin'" because what else can you say? You have no experience with girls. The remainder of high school stretches before you like an infinite desert with no water in sight. You would give anything to be older than sixteen, to be anyone but you, to be anywhere but Scranton, Pennsylvania.

This is how the century is born.

APRIL

Keith Tedesco nonchalantly announces during gym class that he has broken up with Annie. This is earth shattering. This divides all of space and time into two distinct sections: B.A. and A.A.—Before Annie and After Annie. When prodded for further explanation, Keith cryptically says "she wouldn't give it up" before messing around with a basketball. You know what giving it up means despite never having gone on a date. This is when you first begin to fear you will die alone.

In the time of A.A., Keith grows distant and reckless. At first, you believe the breakup will help you dramatically. You assume Keith will now be on the prowl for ladies—you are not sure what this entails but you think it might involve cruising the mall for freshmen. Instead, Keith begins sleeping in his Prelude all the time and rarely wants to drive. One night Keith jumps the gorge at Nay Aug park, a feat you would never try, a stunt you know has killed some dumb luck teenager once a season since before your parents' time.

After the gorge, Keith invites you over and smokes pot while stealing sips of rum annexed from his father's liquor cabinet. You drink cola and feel like a turd. The two of you watch *Terminator*, then *Terminator 2*. You are reassured by the post-human landscape described in these films. The opening credits sequence shows a mechanical skull outlined by fire and you desperately hope for this to happen: for everything organic to be engulfed in flames and replaced with steel, but you can't articulate any of this and instead yell "dang" whenever Arnold Schwarzenegger does something impressive like hurling a biker onto a griddle. Elaine passes by, holds her nose, and calls you dweebs. She wears ribbons in her hair with Bishop O'Hara stenciled in glitter down the sides. She sashays out of the room, and it takes everything you have to hide your veiny boner.

When *T2* ends, Keith talks wistfully of the Uncanny Valley, a scientific theory hypothesizing that whenever CGI characters or robots look too human, people feel a terrible revulsion. He tells you about a Norwegian scientist's recent declaration that the human race is only thirty years away from immortality, that all it will take is nanobots injected into bloodstreams and cyborg enhancements. He tentatively asks you what his funeral would be like. If Annie would weep over his dead body and wish she'd let him inside of her. If any of those Bishop O'Hara bastards would ever call him "faggot" again. You have no idea. You make a mental note to light an extra candle for your only friend.

This is how the century is born.

Inexplicably, Keith stops returning your phone calls. PreludeMan84 is never online. Your parents ask why you no longer go out. You say you don't know, that you don't care, and listen to the same two-dozen CDs for the millionth time. Everything is boring and stupid. You pray to God for more friends and light three candles at church instead of two. You want to know why you are burdened with being so strange.

Keith shows up at your house with a package of cheap fireworks and two forty ounce bottles of malt liquor. You are ecstatic but do not show it. You pretend nothing has happened. You say, "What up, homes?" Keith asks you to come light fireworks at Lake Scranton. He sets them off with his zippo and they are all unimpressive. He becomes drunk halfway through his forty while you nurse your own. The sun sets over the lake and something about this day—the unexpected return of Keith, the fireworks, the first sips of booze—fills you with an anguish similar to the Uncanny Valley. Something here is not right, this lake, this reunion, this life. You remember that barely seen white van coming alongside of you so many years ago, and it feels like a summation of your entire life: sitting oblivious in the backseat while the engine of your destruction rushes onward to meet you.

Keith throws the empty bottle into the lake. It bobs for a few seconds then dips down into the water and drowns. You are sitting on the edge of a stone wall when Keith looks at you and says that he is gay.

You remind him about Annie, how she wouldn't put out. But he tells you no, that it was all a lie, that she wanted to go further and Keith didn't feel like it. You tell him you go to Catholic school, that no one can know, that no one can ever know, that you're going to pretend this never happened, that Keith should do the same. Doesn't he know that being gay is a sin? A mortal sin that leads to ETERNAL DAMNATION? Keith asks if you understand how much harder everything is for him and you say no, because it's not, because he is straight, because everything is fine. A duck hoots on the lake. You walk home alone through two miles of forest.

This is how the century is born.

JULY

Keith calls from time to time. He sends you the occasional instant message. You do not respond and cannot imagine what life will be like from here on out. Without Keith, you have no support system. Bishop O'Hara will be unbearable. But in many ways you are already gone, reading college brochures at night. This is temporary, you tell yourself, this is temporary. Scranton will pass and you will be new and beautiful and wonderful, and no one will ever know about PreludeMan84 or Bishop O'Hara. You go with your parents to the same beach you've vacationed at yearly since birth. They see no need for variation. The beach. The beach. The beach.

On the third day, your parents get a call on the hotel room phone. You find this strange because it has never happened before, and everything else in Ocean City is a series of annual, boring events. But you do not care because there is nothing to care about ever. You are upset because you forgot your CD player at home and can't lose yourself for hours at a time in your collection of burned discs. Your parents tell you a genuine tragedy has occurred. Keith fell asleep in his car with the engine on. He was in the garage. He is dead.

Your parents tell you it was an accident but you know

better. They offer to go home early but you say no, it's fine, and you stay another two days. You wade out into the still ocean and try to see how long you can stare at the sun. The sand is gray. You know that if you remained friends with Keith, you could have prevented his death. You could have made him realize that Bishop O'Hara would not last forever, that in college he could have been reborn. But you did none of these things and feel directly responsible for his death. You wonder what's the most damning sin: homosexuality or murder by neglect.

This is how the century is born.

You wear a too-big dress shirt with a tie meant for school. You wear slacks. You go to the viewing and hug Keith's mother, a caring woman, a doppelganger of your own mother, and she's crying so hard and you feel so guilty and you want to admit everything but you can't. You hug Elaine and it takes everything you have not to get hard in her sloppy embrace, to stop from burying your face in her dark hair, those small, wonderful breasts that seem to contain all the mysteries of the universe. A fly buzzes in the heat and lands on Keith's too-pink cheek.

You will not be able to talk about any of this. You will have to find a device to get around talking about this.

When everything is over, you go behind the building and find Elaine bent behind a dumpster, her cheeks red and tear-stained, a cigarette dangling between her fingers. The ash is long and hangs precariously. She looks up and offers you a drag. Cough, cough, cough. Her long black skirt will occupy a holy recess of your memory forever.

You want to ask Elaine if she had any idea that Keith was gay, because if she doesn't, you know you are scot-free and that no one will ever have to know. You are positive Keith wouldn't have told anyone else the truth. Instead, Elaine says you've both been taught your entire lives that God has a plan for everyone. She tells you this time God was wrong.

For the first time you really question whether or not that's true: the whole God having a plan thing. Losing your faith is not like flipping a light switch. It doesn't happen all in one go. But years later, when your journey from whole-hearted believer to heathen is complete, you will remember this moment huddled in the alleyway behind the funeral parlor. You will remember it and think, "That's where all this shit started." All the questioning, all the doubt. The Death of Keith Tedesco.

This is how the century is born.

SEPTEMBER

The school holds an assembly on September 1st. They say this year will be in remembrance of Keith, that everything the students, faculty and staff do will be living prayers in his honor. Ten days later the Twin Towers fall. On September 12th, you return terrified to the classroom. Keith is forgotten. You sit in the back and sneak glances out the window, waiting and hoping for the end to burn everything clean.

Your English teacher suggests you talk about what happened. No one raises a hand. You mumble something. She asks you to elaborate. You tell her you hope the bad guys don't get Blockbuster because you want to rent video games after school. She says she understands your way of dealing with things is by making fun, but this is the one thing you can never make fun of. You take offense in memory of Keith, how one tragedy can obliterate another.

The part that stings you the most, the scene that will haunt you for years, occurs at home, at night, on the internet.

You sign onto instant messenger during the aftermath of 9/11 and there he is, PreludeMan84. You are shocked. You press your face to the screen. You get as close to Keith as you can.

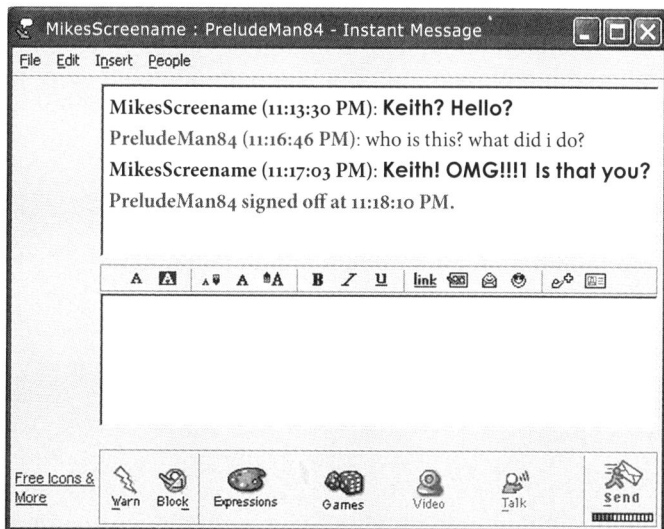

```
MikesScreename : PreludeMan84 - Instant Message        [_][□][X]
File   Edit   Insert   People
─────────────────────────────────────────────────────
  MikesScreename (11:13:30 PM): Keith? Hello?
  PreludeMan84 (11:16:46 PM): who is this? what did i do?
  MikesScreename (11:17:03 PM): Keith! OMG!!!1 Is that you?
  PreludeMan84 signed off at 11:18:10 PM.


  A  A   A  A  A   B  I  U   link           link
─────────────────────────────────────────────────────




─────────────────────────────────────────────────────
Free Icons &                                          Send
More       Warn  Block  Expressions  Games  Video  Talk
```

You can't sleep. Logic dictates that it's one of Keith's parents confused by Instant Messenger, but you hope he's still out there somewhere, that the Bible is wrong, that there is no Heaven, no Hell, only this:

the digital remains, the digital soul, the digital graveyard.

Michael Bishop Falls for
the Second Time

A few weeks after the Potluck Dinner, I finally agreed to meet Ivy's parents for a home-cooked meal at the Chase abode. But first, I had to get through work. Sometimes when I rode the bus to Digital Deluxe with my Orson Welles bio and bagged lunch—egg salad on multigrain, chocolate chip granola bar, key lime pie yogurt—I'd watch the Pittsburgh skyline recede over the river and wish I could travel back in time and reveal to my teenage self all the wonders and accomplishments the future held. My job at Digital Deluxe might have been a sticking point, but even that could be explained away to a younger me. I would tell him in a deep voice: "You're going to live in a real city. You'll ride buses. You'll listen to awesome music. You'll still go to the comic book store every week to read *Ultimate Spider-Man*. Girls will let you ejaculate inside their soft, wonderful vaginas." I flipped through those glossy photos of Orson—so fresh, so clean—in the director's chair on the set of *Citizen Kane*. Who would have thought that a working class boy from Scranton, Pennsylvania could make it in the big city of Pittsburgh? How brave! How noble! How strong!

At Digital, I settled at my desk and for a few minutes agonized over my dinner with the Chase clan later that day. After I worried for what felt like a suitable amount of time, I maximized Facebook and posted Kanye lyrics on my profile. Then, I cruised on over to my web comic and checked the entry I'd uploaded earlier that week.

Lasandra Prochaska *says*:
March 28, 2008 at 3:37 am

We didn't want 2 tell you this but your girlfriend needs a bigger, meatier cock. Give her the almighty schlong she craves. Click here for the sexy & erotic details.
     Fuckably yours,
     Lasandra

CeraLuver1993 *says*:
March 29, 2008 at 9:56 am

Your comics used to really make me laugh. Now there just depressing. What gives? XOXO

Lasandra had pestered me about the size of my penis for so long that I now looked forward to her continued degradations with the anticipation some reserved for half-off weekends at the vintage clothing store. Occasionally, I even responded to the Big L, asking her where she found her information, if she had any incriminating photographic evidence, if she was a scorned ex-girlfriend reincarnated into an internet troll. But CeraLuver1993's—a long time reader but first time poster—three sentence declaration dampened my already wavering spirits. The idea that some fifteen-year-old girl—I inferred as much from the '93 in her handle and the implied love for awkward teen poster boy Michael Cera—eagerly consumed the adventures of my robotic analogues made my heart swell up with something pure and unnamable. But that this same girl would rise from the faceless masses of my two hundred readers and lament the current direction of the series dug at my artistic sensibilities. I looked around my cubicle for answers and only found my Dilbert calendar. Dilbert had forgotten to refill the office printer with toner. Hyjinx ensued.

Junie Censulla doddered through the makeshift maze of cubicles in a tight black dress. "Hudelson wants to see you in his office, Bishop."

I gulped. Then I realized what a cartoony expression this was and immediately regretted it. I tried to reassert my authority by leaning back in my chair and placing my hands behind my head '80s executive style. Then I yawned in Junie's mean, dumb face.

"Oh, sure. Well I've got some important… work to finish. I'll head over in two minutes."

When Junie left, she didn't make that familiar b-line over to her receptionist's desk. Instead, she went straight for the hallway and into Noah's office, the door clicking shut behind her. Like so many other things in the world, this filled me with panic. I'd known Noah long enough to assume he'd never do anything like take a bj from Junie during work, but seeing their continued flirtations spooked me regardless. Yesterday, Noah had uploaded a new video in his series of how-to-basketball thingies, and the only comment came from a YouTube user suspiciously named Jecretary.

Great video! And the host is a total cutie!

Jecretary   19 hours ago   Reply

Ugh. That had to be Junie. I tried to put the engagement out of my mind. I tried to forget how I'd implicated myself in Noah's infidelities. This was not a time for reflexivity or self-examination. I had a middle-aged manager to face by the spine-tingling name of Hudelson.

I called on my vast reserves of strength and fortitude and made the death march to Hudelson's dumb glass office. He was drumming his desk with two pencils when I entered, his eyes closed tight, a look of concentration on his face. I cleared my throat.

"Ah, Michael," he said. "Sit down."

When I sat down, Hudelson stood up and turned his back to me, gazing out at the river. His suit was a nasty beige color and a loose thread hung from the bottom of his jacket. I resisted the urge to reach across the desk and yank on it, maybe push him careening through the glass and onto the street below. Then I'd turn to the proverbial camera and triumphantly shout, "That's how you make street pizza, motherfucka'!" *Michael Bishop Lays a Smackdown on Modern Society: Hyperbole—Sex—Death*, Coming this Summer!

But Hudelson never gave me the opportunity to strike. "We've known each other a long time now haven't we, Michael?"

I checked my watch. I needed to submit a Proof Two of the *Southland Tales* director's commentary before five. "We sure have," I said.

"We sure have. And you know what I've always thought about you, Michael?" He folded his arms across his chest. "I've always thought, 'Hey, there goes Michael Bishop. There's an amigo who takes a lot of pride in his work.' Would you say that's an accurate assessment? Are you the type of amigo who takes a lot of pride in his work?"

"Oh, most definitely. Definitely an amigo of sorts."

He retrieved a thick yellow file from his drawer. He spread it open on the desk and selected a single photocopied page. "That's not what this says, brother. That's not what this says at all." He cleared his throat. "I got a call from Bangladesh today. Madhuri Bahl had to bust my balls because Lionsgate had to bust her balls about the subtitles on *Tyler Perry's Why Did I Get Married*. Do you know what that means? That means I got to bust *your* balls."

I racked my brain for any memories of *Why Did I Get Married*, one of the few Tyler Perry vehicles where he didn't dress up as some African American grandmother. But there was nothing. I sat through eight hours of television and movies a day, five days a week. It all bled together.

"Madhuri explained to me," Hudelson continued, "that there's a scene in the film where Beyonce's song 'Flaws and All' plays over the action. You know we have strict rules concerning subtitles and music. We only subtitle music if it's diegetic. We never subtitle background music. Do you know about this rule, Michael?"

I'd worked there for years. Of course I knew the diegetic rule—if a character sings, we subtitle it; if it's background music, we don't—but wasn't everyone entitled to a screw up now and again? What did they expect, the Jesus Christ of DVD Subtitles?

"Yes, I knew about it."

"Then why didn't you follow it, Michael, because I'm sorry, but we've got a couple hundred thousand newly minted DVDs with non-diegetic music subtitled. And let me tell you, Lionsgate and the Tyler Perry people are not happy. They are not happy one iota. When a studio chooses Digital Deluxe, they're choosing us because of our deluxe quality. It's right there in the name. They're not choosing us because of non-diegetic subtitles. We're not Digital Non-Diegetic." He paused and stroked his chin. "I'll tell you what. If I were you, I would avoid Tyler Perry at all costs. Seems like a funny guy, but I reckon he could take you down in one punch, maybe two max. You're not a big guy, huh? What are you, one-fifty, one-sixty tops?"

I ignored this jab and tried to remember where I'd saved my resume on my laptop. I hadn't updated that loathsome sestina in years, and the thought of sprucing it up seemed like the kind of gargantuan undertaking that could take down someone as powerful as the Mighty Thor or even the *World War Hulk* incarnation of the Incredible Hulk, the one that nearly cracked Earth in half just by walking, the one his alien slave army dubbed The Worldbreaker.

"So here's the deal. Lionsgate has chosen to move ahead with the non-diegetic subtitles but you're going to have to go in, today, before you do the rest of your work, and fix them for future prints. Don't think you can just skip to the Beyonce scene and delete them. I want a full redo of the subtitles just to be safe. That means you might have to stay late tonight. Also, you know there's been talk about gutting the Pittsburgh subtitling department, basically you, and although we're not at that crossroads just yet, things don't look good, Michael, not good at all. And this certainly hasn't helped. I've talked to your supervisor in Bangladesh and we've decided to put you on six month probation with a ten percent pay cut. This isn't the Pirates, kiddo. You don't get three strikes. One more and you're out of here."

Sometimes when I'm presented with too much stimuli and can't possibly respond to everything at once, I open a little drawer inside my buzzing brain and store particularly harmful elements for later consumption. I smiled impotently at Mr. Hudelson before returning to the bright cubicle pit that was the Digital Deluxe Pittsburgh Headquarters. I sat at my computer and tried to envision a world without iPods and Dells and Fords and Blackberrys and our complex web of machines, but even my imagination was barren and projected nothing but the feeble representations I'd seen in countless medieval movies or all those *Final Fantasy* games I'd played as a kid. Even my daydreams about a world without machines were generated by machines. I searched for the *Why Did I Get Married* video file, nervous that Tyler Perry was out to get me, that he'd put on his grandma suit and crash through the window and totally wreck my shit hardcore ninja style. At noon, when Noah stopped by and told me that Sloan had ridden the bus here and did I want to grab lunch at the Double Wide, I said yes, knowing full well that I'd make an already long day even longer, that I'd doom myself to being late for dinner with Ivy's parents.

I did all of this while watching Junie Censulla answering calls at her desk, her expression one of honest-to-goodness pain.

We ate at the Double Wide, a restaurant so corny, so unspeakably tasteless that it looped around and became absolutely breathtaking. The outside was made to look like a 1950s drive-up style restaurant despite the fact that cramped East Carson didn't allow for an actual parking lot. The inside was all stainless steel and mass produced retro novelties. Nothing vintage. Everything shiny and new and processed. Like some nightmare version of Big Boy. Everything on the menu had its own oversized picture surrounded by salivating cartoon wolves.

Sloan clung to Noah's arm. They pressed together, Noah

looking uncomfortable in his slightly wrinkled polo, his Digital Deluxe badge pinned crooked across his heart. Sloan's engagement ring glimmered under the fluorescent lighting and I hoped this wouldn't be the status quo from now on: Oz AWOL in his little world of bits and lasers, Ivy charming but struggling to gain a foothold in our group, me the perpetual third wheel to the tightening fist of Sloan's eternal romance with Noah Black. It was like she'd developed some kind of Spider-Sense for Noah's unsavory desires and had magically appeared at Digital before things could progress any further. If The Engagement had achieved anything, it had glued Sloan to Noah's hip, turning her less interesting, provincial and even somewhat dull. They shared a monstrous sandwich that stunk up the place with its fried onions and slick slices of bacon.

"So," I said, "the engagement. You guys set a date or anything like that?"

Noah took a long, angry bite from their sandwich, momentarily removing himself from the conversation and delegating the task of responding to Sloan, a deer-in-headlights look on her face.

"A date? No. Not yet. We're thinking next year. Maybe the summer. But a winter wedding would be pretty and original."

Noah talked with his mouth full. "Maybe two years. And you never know, if the Republicans win again…" He trailed off.

I didn't understand. "Oh, I totally understand."

A plasma television overhead blared out a recap of that week's NASCAR event. The noise of engines and yee-hawing overpowered Noah tearing at his sandwich like an animal. I nibbled my burger and concentrated on drinking.

"You really going to meet Ivy's parents tonight?" Sloan asked.

I nodded apprehensively. I couldn't think of a single girl

I'd dated that Sloan had approved of, let alone liked. She always had something backhanded to say, like, "She's a babe, but I think you're going to grow tired of her," or the classic, "She's nice, but is that really the type of person you want to associate yourself with romantically?" I thought maybe Ivy would be different since Sloan had known her forever, but Noah knew better and jumped to my rescue, attempting to steer the conversation towards his YMCA basketball team and their playoff prospects. That's when it became clear he'd only invited me to act as a buffer between himself and Sloan's sudden and uncharacteristic neediness. She picked at their shared side of potato salad and slid her arm around Noah's shoulders. She would not be silenced by the reified world of biddy basketball.

"I remember going over her house as a girl," Sloan said. "Ivy Chase? After gymnastics? She had one of those rec rooms instead of a basement and her mom would let us bake with her and make brownies and lemonade. We used to go downstairs and pretend we were a million miles under-ground. Mole people. Her dad's a total freak though. The Jerry Falwell of Pittsburgh, no doubt."

"He can't be that bad."

"Bombed an abortion clinic. Spat on a homosexual dur-ing a gay pride day. Voted for W. twice." She paused to study her reflection in a spoon. "Ok. I made that part up. Maybe not the Bush part, but still. A pastor of some kooky Christian sect. And how about that girl Ivy dragged along to the pot-luck? Elaine something? She was odd too. What was up with that job of hers?"

I looked down at my plate. Elaine. She'd added me on Facebook and I'd accepted, but I hadn't written anything on her wall out of fear she'd bring up going for coffee again. Who knew what an Epidemiologist would want to ask the best friend of her dead younger brother? I didn't intend on finding out.

"I mean really," Sloan continued. "Do you really want to date a pastor's daughter?"

"Don't meddle." Noah spoke with his head down, his hands kneading that sandwich with love and adoration. I hoped this wasn't their home life, Sloan prattling on about whatever random subject came to mind while Noah devoted his full attention to various cuts of meat.

Sloan scooted to the edge of the red vinyl booth and fit the little dip of her chin into her fist. Stock cars roared over-head and we listened to the Home Depot Toyota Camry take the lead. "You boys think whatever you want. Just remember that I tried to warn you. Sometimes you fall in love with the wrong people."

The waitress hurried over with the check, but I wasn't quite ready to let this drop. I wanted to feel more buzzed than I actually did. I wanted this whole terrible day to burn. Mr. Hudelson. My ten-percent pay cut. Sloan and Noah's new dynamic. Tyler Perry. All of it.

"I don't fall in love with the wrong people, S."

She laughed. She dug in her purse for a pair of sunglasses and put them on, making it impossible to gauge her expression. "I didn't mean you specifically, I meant everybody. I meant the entirety of the human race."

I glanced at Noah to see if he'd noticed this comment, if he found it strange or alarming or if he filed it away for further thought. But no, he sat in the booth and devoured his sandwich, paying very little attention to either of us. I wondered if he knew I'd slept with her, but of course I could never ask. We waited for our credit cards and listened to the winning race car driver thank his legion of sponsors—Home Depot, Polaris, Adidas, Whisky River, Unilever, Delphi—the men and women who made physical the products of our dreams.

Late!

Late! Late! Late! Late! Late! Late! Late! Late! Late! Late!
Late! Late! Late! Late! Late! Late! Late! Late! Late! Late!
Late! Late! Late! Late! Late! Late! Late! Late! Late! Late!
Late! Late! Late! Late! Late! Late! Late! Late! Late! Late!
Late! Late! Late! Late! Late! Late! Late! Late! Late! Late!

The Tyler Perry redo took me ninety minutes and as for *Southland Tales*? Well let's just say there's three and a half hours I'll never get back. Ivy told me to be there by six and even though I texted her and explained I'd be late, that still wasn't good enough. The Chases refused to eat without me. They'd let everything go cold before they were rude to a guest. So I booked it out of Digital at six-fifteen and was parked and ready outside the Chase Family Abode only thirty minutes late.

And yet…

There I was. Sitting in my Saturn surveying my features in the rearview like some kind of pre-pubescent narcissist. I studied the contours of my face, the newly set in lines across my forehead, and took in Ivy's sprawling residential development, the flat yards, the towering brick houses. I'd driven there to pick Ivy up before—she still used that tired "I'm staying over Sloan's" excuse, and even if her parents were mentally handicapped they must have deduced the truth behind our rabid fucking—but I'd never actually ventured inside one of the model homes. And so my patented working class shame rose up in my throat like stomach acid.

It had been years since I'd worried about things like class, since I'd traded the papered walls and mining subsidence of Scranton for the University of Pittsburgh, for kids who drove daddy's Beamer and flew home instead of bussing simply because the thought of sitting in a cramped, smelly sardine can for nine hours horrified them to their yuppie-bred cores. I'd endured years of meeting friends' parents and trying not to show my shock at how totally their homes dwarfed my parents'. And I'd come out the other side, proud of my heritage. I'd landed a job that paid ok even in spite of the ten-percent Tyler Perry cut, and I didn't work with my hands—unless you count using a keyboard. But maybe all that newfound confidence was due to my friends living in crap apartments that resembled my own, that in your mid-twenties you rarely meet any of your contemporaries' parents. I palmed sweat on my knees and unlocked the car, feeling sixteen again visiting my first girlfriend. The sinking realization that she lived in the rich neighborhood tucked away in the mountains, a fifteen minute drive from Scranton and its dilapidated mall and muted turf wars. That old fear returned: that I would never be good enough for anyone, that I would never amount to anything during my brief stay in the world.

Ding-dong!

I stood at the front door and studied a small rock pond. The weather had begun to warm, the anticipation of April, the temperature tentatively climbing, climbing, climbing. The ice on top of the pond must have just melted because at its bottom bobbed a slash of white and orange. I knelt down. Was that a dreamsicle or a dead koi? I remembered a photo Oz had sent me on Facebook of Martin Luther King holding one of those delicious orange treats, the text "I Have a Dreamsicle" bold at the bottom.

Mr. Chase opened the door and found me knees bent, shoulders hunched, inspecting the koi holocaust in his front yard. I shielded my eyes from the setting sun and grinned like a deranged lunatic.

"I think your fish is dead." I paused. "Sir."

He smiled that same half-smirk so charming on his daughter. He was built narrow like me, his hair white and cropped close, his eyes sparkling and just barely obscured by rimless glasses. He wore a Lacoste polo shirt and, oh how this put me at ease. That's what I'd worn! A long sleeved one! He looked how I imagined myself in thirty years and I wanted to wrap him up in a great, big bear hug. Oh, please don't hate me, Mr. Chase! I like your daughter ever so much. Validate me! Love me!

First step first. I stood up and shook his hand.

"It's dead?" he asked, referring to the fish. "Troubling. Let's not tell the family just yet. Let's keep this one between you and me. How does that sound?"

"Sounds good, Mr. Chase."

"Mr. Chase is in Arlington Cemetery. Call me Donovan."

"Ok, Donovan."

No other girlfriend's father had permitted me to use his first name and I took this as a sign of goodwill, that I had crossed some invisible threshold in my dating career. Donovan took hold of my shoulder and steered me into the bright world of wonders that waited beyond his front door and the secretly dead koi. He led me into the dining room where the remainder of his family patiently awaited my arrival. The Chases had already set out the food but had the courtesy to keep lids on everything, sealing in the heat, waiting for me. There was Mrs. Chase, thinner than Ivy, higher cheekbones. But she possessed the same blonde curls—a few strands of gray—and the same ocean blue eyes, her nose slightly upturned. And there was the younger brother Ivy rarely spoke of, a thuggish looking teenager, a mass of muscles and fat. He wore a Pirates cap drawn low over his head and scowled at me, aware that I was the reason he had yet to eat.

Ivy Chase sat beside him and looked at me with such fondness that I assumed I'd stepped into some magical dream, the heartbreaking type that eats away at you when you inevitably wake up. Ivy Chase. Blonde and Aryan and well-mannered. Ivy Chase. Intelligent and corn-fed and everything a greasy wap dago from Scranton could ever dare hope for.

"Family, Michael. Michael, family," she said.

The mother hugged me. She felt bony in my arms, her

hair lacquered in place with spray. Jay nodded in my direction and bopped his head. I wanted them to love me, but for now, I settled on the sights and smells of twice baked potatoes and grilled shrimp, roasted chicken with cherry tomatoes. I sat down and picked up my knife and fork. Ivy slapped my hand with a flick of her wrist.

"Not yet." She pointed to the empty seat on my left. "There's one more."

I heard the steady creak of a worn staircase, then the clicking of heels across hardwood. Elaine Tedesco emerged from the hallway with her hair done up around her head, held together with all sorts of pins and contraptions I couldn't name to save my life. She waved at me and walked confidently to her seat, her chin high in the air like an Egyptian queen.

"I forgot to tell you Elaine was coming for dinner too," Ivy said.

Elaine sat beside me and spread her napkin over her lap. "Donovan just gives the best sermons," she said. "I couldn't refuse a dinner invitation."

Donovan tilted his water in her direction. "My darling, you are too kind."

I held fast to my chair, but I very seriously considered throwing my plate onto the carpet as a distraction so I could dive palm-first through the picture window toward the beautiful escape of my car.

Elaine patted my shoulder. "You never got back to me about coffee."

I almost spat a mouthful of water into her face not unlike shocked sitcom characters when presented with something upsetting. Luckily, I only nodded, said yes, and told her that I was a very busy man with busy things to do who was very, oh so very, busy. Busy!

Things improved when we began to eat, even more so when Donovan took hold of the conversation. He asked me all the standard questions that had once shocked my teen-age self. Now I was older and had met a wide variety of girl-friends' parents. On that tentative first meeting, they always asked the same questions lest they wanted to be scolded by their humiliated daughters later on. I told the family about the University of Pittsburgh, how I edited the school's lit-erary magazine, how I developed ever so much under the tutelage of books and a liberal education. I was perfect boy-friend material. Charming and educated. Then I touched upon Scranton, made it into a joke, that I'd grown up with coal stains on my cheeks and rode the trolley to school.

"Scranton wasn't that bad," Elaine said as she dabbed at her lips with a napkin.

I glared at her.

"Oh, that's right," Donovan said. "You're from Scranton too, aren't you Elaine? Now that Michael's done talking, why don't you tell us all a little bit about yourself?"

Now that Michael's done talking. What was that supposed to mean? I looked to Mrs. Chase or Jay for help, but no such luck. They barely even factored into the conversation, their heads tilted toward their plates. Ivy's mother downed her glasses of red wine with relish, with joy, as if she'd trekked across the desert Moses-style and could only now quench her thirst. Jay didn't eat so much as shovel the food into his mouth, the type of boy who murdered ants with magnifying glasses or tormented little girls for lunch money. I wondered if Donovan Chase ever gazed upon his son in astonishment.

"Oh, I'm pretty much an open book," Elaine said.

Please don't talk about Keith. Please don't talk about Keith.

"I studied microbiology at Kings, did some research in Hershey for a few years, then moved to Pittsburgh when I got my Epidemiologist job." She paused and added, "Pittsburgh's a really nice town. Like a big Scranton."

Donovan nodded approvingly. I wiped the sweat off my forehead with the back of my hand.

"She's selling herself short," I said. "We went to the same high school. Elaine was a few years ahead of me and was pretty much legendary at Bishop O'Hara because of her acting. She starred in all the plays. Really, legitimately talented. You know when you watch a high school performance, you never believe it? You never believe those kids are actually the roles they're supposed to be. You see them as kids acting. Not Elaine. She inhabited her roles." I aimed my fork at her. "What happened with all that?"

I couldn't explain my sudden venom, and my audience didn't comprehend it either. A silence filled the room. I had worked so long at concealing my origins, at sealing them up in some dusty cabinet in a cobwebbed partition of my mind. What right did Elaine Tedesco have to be here?

She smiled. "Well, Michael. You'll understand this in a few more years, but eventually everyone has to let go of their childhood dreams. What good does acting do anyway? My job's tracing the spread of cancer. Isn't that a tangible contribution to the world?"

"Speaking of which," Donovan said, "what are your career plans, Michael? Something with the movies Ivy says?"

I looked at their curious faces. Subtitling Tyler Perry vehicles wasn't very noble when compared to cancer research.

"Don't badger him, Daddy." Ivy said this teasingly, lovingly, and it was clear from the way she looked at him—eyes heavy with sincerity—that she was forever and ever a daddy's girl.

"I'm not badgering him, Ivy dear. I'm just trying to get to know your new beau."

"People don't say beau anymore."

"People don't say a lot of things they should." He said this with a smile, a smirk that reminded me of a thousand college

English professors. The ones from the old school, who didn't care about theories or pedagogies, ones who lived for one thing and one thing alone: drama. The ones I had loved. "So come on, Michael. What do you do?"

"I subtitle DVDs."

"Come again?"

"At a studio. Digital Deluxe? It's on the Southside."

"Oh," Donovan said dryly. "Fascinating."

He returned to his chicken, and for a great while there was only the noise of silverware against plates, teeth tearing into meat. When we finished, Mrs. Chase and Ivy shuffled between table and sink, cleaning up despite our protests to help—Jay notwithstanding, he ducked away to his room to lift weights. Before I could get my hopes up that I'd escaped this visit unscathed, Donovan ushered both Elaine and me into the den. He told us to take a load off, that Ivy would be joining us in a few moments with espresso from their very fine espresso machine. Did we like espresso? Very much so we did.

There was a semi-circle of chairs set in front of an unlit fire place, and Elaine and I sat next to each other listening to the haunting growls of the aforementioned espresso machine. It reminded me of those ghastly ghouls from that beloved '80s arcade game *Ghosts n' Goblins*.

"Michael," Elaine said after a brief silence, "my mother asks about you pretty regularly. Did you know that?"

"Your mother?"

"My mother. Yes."

I nodded. The Widow Tedesco. The Mother of My Dead Best Friend. I'd once known her well but had avoided her at all costs ever since Keith's death. The thought of revealing the truth of her son's suicide terrified me. I twiddled my thumbs and tried to appear nonchalant. I awkwardly winked. "How is she doing?"

"Fine. You were so close with Keith. She links the two of you together in her mind. It's natural for her to be curious about you."

"Sure," I said. "Sure. That's very natural. Sure."

And then, THANK GOD, Ivy entered with a tray and three dainty cups of espresso. I grabbed mine so quickly I almost knocked the other two over. Ivy and Elaine both laughed, a look of female collusion in their eyes.

"So what do we do in the den?" I asked.

Ivy took the seat next to mine. "This is where we pray."

My first reaction was to laugh, but I managed to stifle that impulse into an awkward cough when Donovan Chase reappeared with a pamphlet that looked like it had been produced on a home computer. He sat next to Ivy and took her hand, gave it a fatherly squeeze.

"Before you leave," he said, "Elaine asked if we could all say a prayer for her deceased brother."

Everyone bowed their heads. What choice did I have? Ivy took my right hand, Elaine my left. I clamped down on them both. A floor above us I could hear grunting and the slap of weights: Jay Chase lifting no doubt, just waiting for an opportunity to bust the hell out of Dormont. The only thing I wanted from God was to stop Elaine from revealing to Ivy how close I'd been with Keith.

Donovan closed his eyes. "Lord, do not withhold Your mercy from me, may Your love and Your truth always protect me. For troubles without number surround me. My sins have overtaken me, and I cannot see. They are more than the hairs of my head, and my heart fails within me. Be pleased, oh Lord, to save me. Oh Lord, come quickly to help me."

All I could think about was Keith, what the pressure of Christ had done to him, how it drove him into his car, how his lungs filled up with carbon monoxide, how he chose death over being pigeonholed into a life he was in no way equipped to live. I wanted to spontaneously combust and take the entire Dormont development with me.

"May all who seek to take my life be put to shame and confusion. And Lord, a special request for one Keith Tedesco, brother to Elaine. May You shepherd his soul into Your bounty oh Lord. May You anoint us all with true peace. Amen."

Ivy and Elaine echoed his "amen." I said nothing. When it was over, the Chase clan finally allowed me to leave and return to my ordinary life, a world devoid of zealots and beliefs. Banal pleasantries were exchanged, but before I could escape through the front door, Donovan grabbed me by the shoulder.

"I'd like you to do me a favor, Michael. Not for me, but for Ivy. She may not show it because we've raised her not to be boastful. We've raised her not to rub her faith in other people's faces, especially in this day and age. We know the stereotypes and prejudices. But if you really care about my daughter, I'd like you to come to one of my services at the Church of the Synoptic Gospels. I think you'll find it enlightening."

"Oh, sure," I shouted quickly as I stepped outside. "That sounds great!"

I jogged across the lawn. Ivy waved at me from the porch, her parents standing behind her, their hands on each of her shoulders like some kind of Norman Rockwell madness. I fumbled with my car keys as Elaine passed by. "Don't forget our coffee date!" she called out.

I nodded and entered the car, locked it behind me. I started the engine and sat in the blast of lukewarm air, my spirits low, my ego beaten, bruised. If I closed my eyes I could see the suffocated face of Keith Tedesco. I could see him towering above us, giant-like, wading through the soup of Dormont, through Pittsburgh, eager to show us what waits at the very end of our lives.

The Son of God Complex

On October 23rd, 2003, a then unknown African American drove a rented BMW from Los Angeles toward his makeshift home at the W Hotel. He was twenty-five and had traded his hometown for LA like so many other ambitious young Americans who dreamt of becoming famous. But that dream was almost cut tragically short when the young man fell asleep at the wheel and collided with a white van just a few miles short of his hotel.

He woke up in a hospital lucky to be alive. He was in stable condition, but his jaw would have to be wired shut for six weeks. For forty-two days the only child from Chicago moped around his hotel room. With little to occupy his time, this lapsed Christian began to read his complimentary hotel Bible. He rediscovered God and began to believe that the Almighty had saved him from death for a specific purpose, that he was the inheritor of an important destiny, a modern day savior.

Within one year after the car crash, Kanye West became the most popular rapper on Planet Earth.

Only-children are prone to this type of reaction. They're brought into the world as the sole creation of their parents, much like the Lord Jesus Christ. Often times they can begin to develop delusions that their birth is inherently unique, that unlike the millions of nameless masses, they've been ushered into the world for a reason, a Son of God Complex. What would appear to be luck or happenstance to normal, well-adjusted individuals can appear to be fate or worse, divine intervention, to the only child. They can believe themselves saviors and occasionally in need of saving themselves.

But Kanye West is not a savior without faults. Possessor of a notorious insecurity, most of West's raps are elaborate boasts and hyperbole. His music focuses on how amazing he is, what a champion he is, how everyday folk can't even resist talking about him at barbershops. Kanye uses the rap game to mask his own lack of self-confidence. He grew up the son of an English professor but dropped out of college his freshman year. In retaliation, he wrote and produced a trilogy of albums aimed at leveling the Ivory Tower of higher education. After his fiancé left him and the death of his mother—caused by a botched plastic surgery job paid for by West—he retreated to his Honolulu studio with a Roland TR-808 drum machine and emerged months later with digital proof of his sorrow, the album *808s & Heartbreak*.

But the greatest insight into Kanye's psyche came when pop culture slaughterhouse *South Park* featured West on their show as the only person in the world too dense and self-important to get a simple joke about fish sticks. The real life West couldn't let things go without a response and left a rambling post on—what else?—his blog. For once, Kanye dropped the showboating and admitted that he was working on his ego. He explained that his extreme overconfidence was a way early in his career to build himself up when everybody else wanted to tear him down. He understood that acting that way now—as a Grammy award winning millionaire—was absurd, and he promised his fans that he would become better, that he would be remade brand new.

Despite his claims that he's the greatest human being who ever lived, despite the fact that he not-so-secretly believes his life holds greater meaning than normal people, despite the fact that he turns everything into self-aggrandizing nonsense and ridiculous jokes, beneath is a wounded human being unable to process the world. The rappers Kanye grew up listening to expounded on the external struggle. Kanye has made a career of exploring the struggle within.

Guest Starring: God!

Baseball season started a few weeks after my dinner adventure at the Chase household. Ivy and I marched across the bright yellow Clemente Bridge—swollen with fans, closed to traffic during ball games, saxophone players standing on guard rails belting out recognizable sitcom themes—toward the ballpark for the very first home game. Oz hurried awkwardly behind us. I wore my Nyjer Morgan jersey, Ivy her Freddy Sanchez, and Oz went with a too-tight flannel shirt buttoned straight to his neck. It thrilled me that Ivy loved not the championship prone Steelers or Penguins, but the eternally anemic Pirates, a team so unspeakably awful that any time they approached a five-hundred win percentage was a great boon for the buccaneer faithful. And being outside with hundreds of other Pittsburghers? Well it was something all right. It was nice. And I couldn't help but want to extend that to Oz, to remind him that not everything in life had been ruined by social networking and viral advertising. He'd offered to drive us into downtown—it was so rare to see him take his beater Cavalier out of our garage—and honestly seemed excited over the prospect of doing something outdoors with his peers.

We sat two levels back from home plate. Nine dollar seats. The best view in the city. The outfield ahead of us, then the three rivers and that jagged skyline cocooned by all those bridges. Everything so close it still moved me after seven years, was still impressive to a small-minded Scrantonian who'd grown up across from a highway sound barrier. We ate overpriced hot dogs and drank Yuengling from cans and applied sunscreen to our exposed arms, making everything shiny and new. Oz sulked. When the second inning ended, he started tapping his iPhone, sweat pooling under his armpits.

"Really?" I set my Yuengling in the cup holder. "The iPhone now?"

"You gotta see this new app I got. It's called Baseball Live. It shows any game in the majors in real time. Check it out."

He handed me the slippery screen and there it was, the Pirates versus the Reds done up in a cartoon overlay resembling a Nintendo game. I watched the real life Adam LaRoche swing big and miss on the field, then the digital strike symbol flash on the iPhone.

"Isn't that totally amazing? It's pretty much the best thing ever."

Ivy wasn't listening. She had little patience for gadgetry, and thus, had a low tolerance for Oz. I kept telling her he used to be different, but she had yet to be convinced.

"Do you even like baseball?" I asked him.

"Not really. But now I can watch it on my iPhone. I can tweet about it."

LaRoche hit a grounder and arrived safely at first. The crowd cheered. A moment later so did Oz. He was watching the game on his iPhone despite the digital delay. I didn't know what I could do for him. I thought a beautiful day, a baseball game, being with me and Ivy might help, but clearly it didn't. Clearly someone had to take desperate measures, and it appeared as though that someone might be me. But Ivy was beside me. So distracting, so pretty, my feelings for her so all consuming that Oz was often reduced to an afterthought.

Ivy took my hand. "Do you want to grab an ice cream? Maybe take a walk?"

"Yes," I said. "Yes."

We walked hand-in-hand through the concrete innards of the stadium, the throngs of fans united under a single cause. We took our time, occasionally stopping by the tastier seats to watch Morgan and Sanchez, the Pirates striking out three times in succession.

"So," I asked as we waited in line for snacks, "you're really into baseball?"

"Def. It's a gentleman's sport. It's the proletariat's last connection to the ruling class." She paused. "I like the crack of the bat."

"The crack of the bat?"

"Do I stutter?" she asked with a smile.

She pulled her hair into a ponytail. Ivy Chase. My girl-friend. I rocked back and forth on my heels and tried not think about my wreckage of a job, my ruined friends, my multiplying failures hiding in the unknowable future waiting to snatch me away from what little fortune I'd stumbled upon. It was enough for now to be in the ballpark with Ivy Chase all blonde, her skin the color of milk. Ivy Chase of the Natural World, the girl who could rescue me from the fate of Oz who had brutally severed his connection to humanity. Ivy Chase! Ivy Chase!

"I love you," I blurted.

The woman behind the counter waved at me. Her

hairnet shone metallic under the light of the food court. "Next please!"

I watched Ivy. She didn't give me that half-smirk. Her face turned stoic and she nudged me over to the cash register. I lamely requested two chocolate ice creams before Ivy corrected me, told the register jockey she wanted vanilla.

When our order was processed and we'd retreated to the napkin dispenser, I poked Ivy with my elbow. She started at the bottom of the vanilla making a complete lap with her tongue, then started again an inch higher.

"So are you just going to Han Solo me or what?"

"What?"

"Han Solo. At the end of *Empire Strikes Back*?"

She papered her waffle cone with napkins. "I don't remember. Give me some context."

"Han's about to get frozen in carbonite in Cloud City. Then Princess Leia yells that she loves him and he just gives her this tough as nails badass look and says, 'I know.' I didn't even get an 'I know.'"

This earned me the half-smirk. She busied herself with her ice cream and took a big old bite off the top. I envied people who could do that. The cold always stung my teeth.

"I know," she said.

Something in my face must have given me away. I prided myself on never letting girls, never letting anyone, know that I had the capacity of being hurt, that I had actual human feelings. I hid my face behind my ice cream like a first grader with a crush.

"I'm just slow, ok?" She patted my arm. "I care about you a lot. I do. But there's still so much we don't know about each other. Half our conversations are you trying to make me laugh."

"I'm not trying. I'm inherently hilarious."

"My dad asked you to come to one of his services. That

was like what, a month ago? You haven't even tried. At least Tommy humored him."

"The carpenter? You guys only dated two months."

"We've only dated three."

And so there it was: an impasse. She'd compared me unfavorably to her ex-boyfriend. Absence makes the heart grow fonder and all that garbage. My ice cream started to melt down my hand. She pulled another napkin from the dispenser and wiped me clean before tossing it into the trash chute built right into the counter. Where did that go anyway? Was there an unseen garbage bag underneath or maybe a pipe that went underground? A network of tunnels filling with human waste?

"Tomorrow. I'll go to your father's service tomorrow," I said.

"Good. I'd hug you but there's ice cream between us."

When I returned home that night I couldn't sleep. I'd taken Ivy back to Dormont and there was nothing good on TV, nothing left in my Hulu queue. Around two in the morning, I surfed over to Facebook and resumed my vanity project. It had started innocently enough when I'd uploaded that first picture of Keith and me smiling in front of his Honda Prelude. But in the intervening months, during the initial bloom of my love affair with Ivy Chase, I had begun to build a Facebook profile for the deceased, the missed, the dead: Keith Tedesco.

Login: Keith Tedesco
Password: You_are_a_sick_fuck_Michael_Bishop

There was his sixteen-year-old face. I cropped it from the aforementioned picture. So far I'd set his profile to the maximum privacy limits, meaning that if someone searched for him, all they would see was his name, not even a picture. Keith Tedesco truly was a digital ghost. As I sat there in the dark, I didn't feel guilty or anxious. Hadn't I suffered enough? Hadn't I shouldered the burden of Keith's secret life all by my lonesome for so very, *very* long? Didn't someone owe me this?

I tagged him in a handful of pictures. Nothing serious. I had yet to cross any line I couldn't double back upon later. Look at Keith at Semi with Annie! Look at Keith at eighth grade graduation with the already stunning Elaine! I filled out his Personal Information. Keith's favorite activities involved "being kind to others, not degrading people to make me feel better about myself, standing up for what's right, having a backbone, not lying to my friends." Maybe Keith wouldn't have chosen these words to describe himself, and maybe, in a few cases they didn't even apply. No matter! I was the one in charge here, and in my perfect Facebook universe, this was the person Keith had been.

I updated his status.

Keith Tedesco is happy and fulfilled. He is devoid of anxiety and fear and indecision. He is the type of person you wish you could be.

I'm sure that many of my friends would think I was the biggest creeper ever, and at the very least I'd have trouble sleeping after fiddling around with my dead buddy's online avatar. I didn't. I shut off my phone and stretched out naked in bed, holding the weight of the comforter against my chest and imagining it as Ivy's body. I fell asleep instantly, so fully, so completely, that you would have thought it impossible for anyone to reach that level of unconsciousness without really being dead.

The next morning, I awoke to a wealth of cryptic messages from my dear and wonderful friends. Ivy and I had sex after the Pirates game, so I cruised on over to Facebook to see if she'd posted any status updates commenting favorably or unfavorably on my sexual technique, or more importantly, if she left behind any clues about who she really was at her core.

Ivy Chase is like the blue jay in the yard: light and full of air!

And…

Ivy Chase is reminded of the importance of juice after a long workout the night before.

I decided those updates could go one way or the other—because although it was true that our sex the night before had tenuously approached the hour mark, that was only after Ivy got a game of tennis in at the courts on Wightman. I logged off and turned on my phone. Both Noah and Sloan had tried and failed to get in touch with me. First, a text from Noah Black:

Hey. Meeting up w/Junie. Told Sloan that me and you are playing Nintendo. If she calls just lie.

Then these gems from Sloan Smith on my voicemail:

Beep.

Hi, friend. This is S. Just seeing how you're hanging. Boys' night and all that.

Beep.

Hi again. I just picked up a six-pack at Kelly's. Is Noah still there? Want to all split it? Neither of you are answering so I assume you're playing through Ducktales *again. If you want some beers, just call me. I'll come over. I'm just hanging.*

Beep.

Are you there? Why won't anybody answer me?

I showered. I brushed my teeth. I washed my face 1,700 times just like my dermatologist suggested years earlier after inspecting my acne with a miniature lightsaber. In short: I did all the things that modern men are expected to do when preparing to see their significant other's father deliver a sermon. But I was distracted. I wasn't sure who aggravated me more, Sloan or Noah. On one hand, when did Sloan devolve into such a sniveling girlfriend? She'd always been more like a guy, the love 'em and leave 'em type. How had she been reduced to this, the type of woman who spent her days tracking her beau like some kind of lame Dick Tracy? And Noah? Christ. Not telling Sloan about his indiscretions in the past had been bad enough, but now that they were engaged? Gross. I did not want to be implicated. I did not want to be held accountable for anyone's sins but my own. For the first time, I began to consider the ramifications of telling Sloan the truth.

I put on a tie but kept it loose around my neck, didn't button the top button. It was a look I was developing called Nonchalant Elegance. I toasted an English muffin, fried an egg, and tucked it inside beneath a slice of low-fat Swiss cheese. In the living room, the furniture had all been moved. The futon and couch pressed against the wall. The table upside down on the floor. I figured it was Oz sleepwalking again and sat down in the kitchen to eat. He found me there a few moments later paging through a fifteen-year-old issue of *Amazing Spider-Man*.

"Rearrange the furniture again last night?" I asked.

"Yeah. It's no big deal." He burped loudly while scratching his plaid boxer shorts. "What are you dressed up for?"

"Ivy's dad is a pastor and I said I'd see him do mass or whatever."

He went into the kitchen and pulled a box of Captain Crunch off the fridge. He ate them by the handful. "Why?"

"I don't know. It's important to her."

"That's retarded." He munched another handful. "How's Peter?"

"Who?"

He pointed at the comic.

"Spidey? Fine. He's hanging with his clone. Ben Reilly. Remember him? Named after Ben Parker and Aunt May's maiden name?"

"Sure. Hey, listen. Why don't you blow off this Jesus thing and the two of us can go into Oakland and check out the comic store. Get some trades. We haven't done that in forever."

It broke my heart to see Oz this way, trying to act like it was the olden days, like we were twenty-year-olds wreaking havoc, scamming anyone we could for sips of whiskey and forties of Miller High Life. He'd never been one to request help and I knew this was as close as he'd get, as near as he'd come to telling me he needed a friend, that he needed help, that he realized all those days hidden in the stacks of Hillman Library were eroding his humanity, were causing him to wander around the house in his sleep. And to be honest, I really wanted to go with him, to ditch Ivy and her father and spend the day drinking coffee in Oakland and poring over the comic store's one-dollar back issue bins—like the Flash and his cosmic treadmill, could I too travel back in time? But we weren't twenty anymore and I selfishly prioritized Ivy's happiness over Oz's mental wellbeing.

"I can't." I finished the egg sandwich. "But let's hang out tomorrow. Or the day after that? What do you say?"

He shrugged, said no big deal, and retreated into his bedroom. Then the noise of his keyboard, his fingers loud as they hammered out meaning.

I didn't know then that within twenty-four hours he'd be gone.

The GPS yelled at me. It was new, a birthday gift from my parents, and I couldn't figure out how to control the volume. All I'd managed to learn was how to switch voices. So instead of an American woman, now a British man shouted, "Make a u-turn now! Make a u-turn now! Recalculating!" I veered into a McDonald's and waited at a nearby intersection before doubling back, the GPS flashing red the entire time, my estimated arrival time climbing steadily upward toward infinity.

I probably should have googled directions to the church instead of relying on the GPS, but this was my first real chance to test it out. And how could I pass up the opportunity to drive around guided by our nation's first tentative step toward a robot butler, a futuristic development I'd dreamt about ever since watching all those *Jetsons* reruns as a child? But the GPS sounded so much angrier than I'd imagined—more T-1000 than Rosie—and to make matters worse, its obnoxiously loud voice made it all but impossible to focus on the comic book podcast I'd chosen specifically for this occasion.

So it was with a great deal of frustration that I finally pulled into 820 Matthew Road and discovered that Ivy's father was not a minister of some steepled church as I'd imagined, nothing like those Catholic masterpieces that had won me over in my impressionable youth. Instead, the address Ivy had given me led to a strip mall between two competing gas station franchises, a Sheetz and a GetGo. I cruised into the lot and rechecked my text messages, assuming I'd entered the wrong address into the GPS and would now miss the entire service instead of just the first five minutes. But no, there it was, dated that morning from Ivy. *820 Matthew*. I pulled up to the stores. A Fashion Bug, a Mom and Pop Laundromat, a boarded-up TCBY with a dusty For Rent sign in the window. And there, at the far end of the shops beyond a Dollar

General hung an inconspicuous sign promoting the Church of the Synoptic Gospels, its font plain and black against faded yellow.

The GPS announced I'd arrived at my destination. I thanked it and yanked the power cord, then studied the Church of the Synoptic Gospels. The windows were long and rectangular; they almost reached all the way down to the pavement. They gave a perfect view of the inside, maybe two-dozen people sitting in metal folding chairs arranged in a circle, Donovan Chase standing in the middle, pivoting, gesturing. It reminded me of the studio where I'd taken karate lessons as a child. It reminded me of all those Goodwills I scanned for vintage sweaters.

Inside, everyone went silent and watched me enter. A few smiled, including Ivy and Elaine Tedesco who sat side-by-side. Mrs. Chase had that blank expression she'd worn the entire time I'd eaten dinner with them and Jay wasn't even paying attention. He looked out the window at an old German Shepard that had wandered into the parking lot. It barked at nothing in particular and gave a cursory wag of its tail.

"I see we have a newcomer," Donovan said. He pointed toward the lone empty chair between two women who looked like elderly bag ladies. "Join us, Michael."

I did as instructed, my back slick with sweat. Mr. Chase wore khakis and a plaid button down shirt beneath a navy sweater vest. He looked nothing like the robed priest from my childhood. I folded my hands over my lap, felt self-conscious, and stuck them under my armpits.

"As I was saying," Donovan continued, "I once met a young man who was lost. He came from a good family, enjoyed a great education, but you know what? He was directionless."

One of the bag ladies at my side murmured, "Mmm-hmm," and I just about pissed myself. Did people really say these things? Had I fallen into *Sister Act 2*?

"I don't blame this young man. I really don't. I blame society." He paced while he talked, marching inside that little circle of chairs, his reflection shadowing him in the window like Peter Pan. "Technology run rampant. Cloning. All these terrible celebrities. Reality TV. You can't really blame this young man, because he's not a member of the first generation to grow up without God, he's the second. This generation's proverbial parents are secular, and because of that their children have been lured away from not only religion, but the natural world as well, by technology and sin."

I sat there stunned and tried to smile. He couldn't be talking about me right? I thought about Keith and my bumbling religious childhood and how that fanatical devotion contributed to his suicide. I wanted to reach under my uncomfortable metal chair and pull out a black and gray Nintendo Entertainment System. I wanted to bash Donovan across the head with it, grab Ivy by the hand—maybe even her emotionally comatose mother and that sweetheart of my high school career, Elaine Tedesco—and sprint out of there trailed by explosions. Leap at the last minute from the ensuing fireball and rocket pack across the highway so we could share martinis on the roof of some glorious hover skyscraper.

Instead, I sneezed. Donovan looked in my direction and winked with terrible menace.

"So what I'm suggesting is a turning away from technology, the internet, even television. It will be hard. And it will be gradual. But at the end of the road will be something far more worthwhile than a few Twitters on your phone."

A few members of the congregation laughed. Somebody even elbowed their neighbor like people do at comedy clubs on sitcoms.

"At the end of that road awaits communion with God. A communion with God here on earth. A Christian nirvana if you will. A renaissance for not only the Church of the Synoptic Gospels but for all those who count themselves among

Jesus' faithful. Amen." Donovan returned to the center of the circle and genuflected. "Now. Before we finish up for the day, has anyone made any progress on our public works program?"

An uncomfortable silence followed where no one moved, where time seemed to slow to molasses. Didn't they have enough money for air conditioning? Where's your Moses now as Edward G. Robinson might say. I smiled at my own natural wit, but that grin was short-lived as Ivy pertly raised her hand and spoke in a voice that still had the power to make my heart contract with wonder.

"I was at the soup kitchen last Thursday. I met a man named Franklin. He said he used to tow cars around Robinson but had fallen on his luck because of the economy. I told him about the Church of the Synoptic Gospels, and he promised he'd come next weekend."

Ivy volunteered at a soup kitchen? She'd mentioned "community service" with her family but didn't say it was connected to the church. She wouldn't meet my eyes and I could feel my cheeks go red with shame. What else hadn't she told me?

Then Elaine talked about her progress convincing an RN at work to attend a service. The woman on my left said she'd talked her sister into donating fifty dollars in honor of their deceased and beloved aunt. They went around the room like that and I sat there and tried to tune it all out, to fall back on the familiar strategy I'd employed through that final year of high school theology, to pick a spot on the ceiling and play *Super Mario Bros.* in my head.

Finally, Donovan Chase called the congregation to join him on his knees and give thanks to the Lord. I got down and watched everyone bow their heads and close their eyes. Only Donovan's remained open. Donovan's and mine.

He stared at me for the duration of his "final prayer."

"Dear Lord," he said, "thank You for everything You've

given us, the miracles that are present all around us, the infinite beauties that we miss again and again due to our inherent human failings and our never-ending interest in the misleading drama of the so-called real world. Thank You for delivering unto us the Church of the Synoptic Gospels so that we may serve those who have not let You into their hearts. And thank You for bringing us our visitor today, Michael Bishop, and may You allow him to become a regular fixture here and in our hearts as well. And most of all, thank You for saving us, O Lord. Thank You for saving us."

No one moved when Donovan finished as if the Synoptic believers didn't quite know how to make a break from the world of spirituality and God and return to the mundane tasks of rooting in pockets for car keys, of checking your breath against the back of your palm. It was Donovan who returned to the material world first, Donovan who walked past the group and away from the circle of chairs. He busied himself at the entrance with a small leather book, scribbling away some notes. The others collected their things, and it became clear that Donovan Chase was waiting to shake all our hands just like in real church. I rubbed the back of my neck.

"Hi!"

It was Ivy. Ivy Chase! Blonde and beautiful and full-lipped. I blinked at her.

"Oh?"

"Do you want to go to the Dor-Stop?"

"Uh? What?"

"Great." She touched my arm. "I'll meet you by your car."

I nodded as she hurried out. She gave her father a great big kiss on the cheek. Her mother and brother passed, but neither came over to chitchat. Maybe they were embarrassed. They walked out with their heads hung low, taking what little comfort they could in that they'd survived another service. Or maybe not. Maybe I was just projecting. And then of course was Elaine, a seemingly constant refrain in my life reminding me about our "coffee date" and how she wanted to get down and dirty and dish about her brother. By the time she left, the church had emptied out except for me and the pastor. He flashed his teeth and didn't wait for me to approach. I was still standing by my chair, brain dead and stupefied like a person who walks out of a big budget action movie and is shocked to discover it's nighttime, that the world has not ended in a rocking montage of sex explosions.

"Michael. Michael, Michael, Michael." He pressed his long, narrow fingers into my shoulder. "Glad you could make it. So happy to see you. What did you think of the services here?"

What I wanted to tell Donovan Chase was something I'd hidden even from his daughter: the whole story of how I'd once believed everything the church told me, every last bit of the Bible, but how Keith's death changed all that, how I still felt guilty about my reaction to his coming out. I thought I'd overcome these hang ups. Why was Donovan doing this? Why was he trying to lure me back to the fold? Hadn't we evolved?

"Was that about me back there? Were you talking about me?"

Donovan frowned. "Not anyone specific, Michael. More of a generational observation. But sure, I could see how you might identify with what I was saying. I know you only came along because Ivy asked you to, but faith really means a lot to us Chases. During the week, I work in sales. Our family sacrifices a lot to keep the lights on here. We'd love it if you became more involved."

I stammered something indecipherable while Donovan steered me toward the exit and the relative safety of the parking lot. Ivy was waiting for me and we entered my car without even saying hello. I buckled myself in, but didn't start the engine. I wanted to get rid of her and jet back to Squirrel

Hill as fast as I could. I thought about *The Legend of Zelda: A Link to the Past*, one of my favorite Super Nintendo games, in which you have the ability to switch between two mirrored worlds: Light and Dark. In the former, you might find a cheery forest or a village populated with friendly townspeople, but if you switched to the Dark and explored the very same area, you'd enter a spooky graveyard or skeleton-filled dungeon. I felt like I'd fallen into the Dark World! That the Ivy Chase I'd grown to care about and even love had been replaced with this cruel doppelganger, this Dark monstrosity who actually bought into something as foul as the Church of the Synoptic Gospels!

"It's really hot out," she whined. "Can you turn on the air or something?"

"The air? The air."

I started the engine. I turned on the air. A couple—one in medical scrubs, the other wearing a Jordan jersey—pushed a shopping cart toward the Dollar General. They were trailed by two children in matching Spider-Man t-shirts and Spider-Man Velcro sneakers. The kids circled each other like lions. What I wouldn't have given to be in their shoes instead of mine.

"So," Ivy said, "the Dor-Stop. You gotta try their raspberry stuffed French toast."

"No, Ivy. I don't want to go to the Dor-Stop."

She clicked in her seat belt. "Why not? What's wrong?"

"I'm a little freaked out right now. I thought your dad was going to pull out snakes or start speaking in tongues. I don't even know what a Synoptic Gospel is."

"They're the three gospels minus John's. Dad broke off from the Protestants because he doesn't believe in John. John is more conservative. John focuses on Jesus' godliness instead of his humanness. And there's nothing about helping the poor or sick. That's emphasized in the Synoptics."

I kept the car in park. "Are you kidding?"

"No. And I don't see why you're making such a big deal out of this. Let's go get brunch."

"A big deal? Ivy, your dad's a lunatic. Do you actually believe this junk? You read. You read!"

"Flannery O' Connor and Leo Tolstoy were both devout Christians. What's your problem today?"

"Nothing. I just haven't met an honest-to-goodness believer since moving here. I'm trying to understand this, but…"

"Do you really think you're the first person who thinks it's weird that I'm a believer? Michael, I've straddled the line between super cool hipster girl and deeply religious pastor's daughter for years. But this is who I am, and I came to terms with that a long time ago. I love books and art and culture and indie music and bars, but I'm also anchored by my faith in Christ." She folded her arms across her chest. "I like you because you're funny and cynical on the surface, but it's so obvious to me that that's just a shield, that beneath all that you're this needy guy who desperately wants to be loved. If you want to be with me, you need to accept my spirituality." She paused. "There's a lot in the Bible that's really helpful on a day-to-day basis. It doesn't matter if it's all literal or if Moses really parted the Red Sea or if Noah collected a pair of every animal on Earth. The morals in those stories are useful. It's a manual on how to live. Religion really helped me when Danielle died. Maybe you need ask yourself why you find it so hard to believe."

I couldn't believe it. She wasn't being ironic at all! Not even in the slightest. Didn't she know you weren't supposed to have these conversations past your freshman year of college? Didn't Ivy Chase understand that no one who grew up in the age of Nintendo, no one who witnessed the rise of Facebook and Twitter could possibly believe in a magic book written under divine inspiration two thousand years ago?

Didn't she know that I couldn't tolerate this kind of

anesthetic mumbo jumbo in the wake of Keith Tedesco's death?

"This makes me think a lot less of you," I said. "I used to think you were really intelligent."

She stared straight ahead, expressionless. A moment passed before Ivy left the car. She didn't slam the door like I expected. She shut it slowly, softly, as if the physical act actually pained her. I watched her walk across the parking lot to god knows where, her feet swollen in high heels. Then I drove home and watched amateur porn on the internet. I'd grown found of amateur solos, videos of perfectly average girls masturbating into shoddy webcams. I liked to gaze into their fluttering eyes and listen to their gentle moans of pleasure. I jerked off into a tube sock and tossed it by a stack of old *Green Lantern* comics I was rereading. I didn't picture Ivy Chase when I came. I didn't picture God.

The Bedtime Lullaby for a Demographic Doomed

The Sunday after my disaster at the Synoptics, I received a call from my parents while putting the final touches on my latest web comic.

I saved it, pleased with the finished product and its over-the-top malaise. I hadn't told my parents about Ivy and when asked explained we were going through a rough patch, that I had "problems with her spirituality," that we hadn't seen each other since I told her off in the Saturn.

"But she's such a pretty girl from the pictures you sent us. So what if she has faith?" my mother asked. "You went to Catholic school. Are you eating well? Are you holding up without her?"

The truth was I'd moped around the house all week drinking whiskey. I'd stopped making meals and started eating stale boxes of Cheez It's for dinner. At work, I'd been assigned the first season of *Tyler Perry's House of Payne* and spent my days paranoid that Perry himself had requested me and was now just waiting for me to screw up so he could pop out of my desk drawer and beat the living tar out of me with his pumpkin-sized fists and monstrous abs.

"I'm swaggin' times a hundred thousand billion."

"What about Oz?" she asked. "How's he?"

Oz.

Oz?

Oz?!

Was it possible that in my narcissistic wallowing over Ivy Chase that I'd forgotten about my best friend? Was it possible that I actually hadn't seen him in a week? Yes. A thousand times yes. I remembered my parents' announcement years ago in Ocean City, that Keith had suffocated, that Keith had died. I knew it was melodramatic even in the moment, but it's the first place my mind went: Oz might be dead. In a way, it felt like I'd been cruising toward this outcome ever since Keith's funeral, that his death was not an outlier but a chorus-verse-chorus I was doomed to repeat. I was a bad friend and this was my fate. I went into the hallway and shouted Oz's name. I checked under the kitchen table and beneath the futon. I ran into the basement and scanned the rafters. I stood outside his bedroom door, my throat constricting with panic, my brain feeling drained of some substantial nutrient. I closed my eyes and took deep breath after deep breath. I silently counted backwards from twenty-five. If something truly terrible had happened, I would have found out by now, I reassured myself. Everything is going to be ok. Everything is going to be ok. This is not happening again. Oz's room looked the same as ever. The floor carpeted in clothes, the bed unmade, the closet door wide open revealing a collection of flannel shirts that would make the ghost of Kurt Cobain envious. A stack of papers, their edges bent and dog-eared, sat on his desk. *The Contact Zone of Countervoices: A Sustainable Ludic Pedagogy in 21st Century Composition Programs by Owen Osborne III.* I flipped through thirty-seven pages of block quotes and screen captures of boring looking flash games, prose like "culpability of the American institution in the post-Twitter era" and "the evolution of textual criticism from the printed page to the inherent constant of play in new forms of subjectivity and disease approach to information as a dynamic network." I didn't understand any of it. But at the end of the paper was that all too familiar paragraph of negative comments culminating in a definitive F. The teacher's language was even more cryptic than Oz's, but I think she understood he wasn't even making sense anymore, that his quest to better understand technology had turned him into a rambling madman. Even his professors could tell he was losing it.

I logged onto Facebook. There was no activity on Oz's profile, only a post from one of his comp students asking why he hadn't come to class and if they were going to get their papers back to revise before final portfolios. I scrolled down and found a YouTube clip he'd posted a week earlier titled *Actual Man is Electrocuted to Death.* The video showed what the title promised: a real live human being dancing on top of a stopped train in broad daylight. While twirling his hands, he accidentally comes into contact with a power line. There's a brief popping noise, a small cloud of smoke, and the man collapses. The crowd screams. The video ends. I watched it ten times. Underneath the clip, Oz had typed *Is this progress?*

The first clue came via Twitter. Above the usual nonsense about ludic pedagogy and masturbatory updates about the subpar sushi in the Cathedral of Learning was the closest thing I had to a lead.

Anti-Oedipus Oz
@AntiOedipusOz

My chances of becoming a great scholar have been dismantled by a cunt who knows nothing about the open system that's engulfing academia.

0	0
RETWEETS	FAVORITES

6 days ago - via iTwitter · Details   ↶ Reply ↺ Retweet ★ Favorite

Anti-Oedipus Oz
@AntiOedipusOz

I have decided that I have been living a lie and can stomach it no longer.

0	0
RETWEETS	FAVORITES

6 days ago - via iTwitter · Details   ↶ Reply ↺ Retweet ★ Favorite

I paced through the house and sat on the ledge of the porch. It was raining lightly and I liked how the cobblestone streets looked when they got wet. I figured I should contact someone, but who? The police? Oz's mother? She was always so frightened that something would happen to her precious baby boy after her husband died over Al Kut. She still sent Oz care packages filled with homemade Rice Krispie squares and an endless array of plaque fighting gum. I would have to call them both eventually, but I wasn't ready yet, couldn't face acknowledging that I'd once again let someone down, possibly with fatal consequences. I tried to put death out of my mind, tried to convince myself that Oz was out there somewhere gallivanting across these United States getting his groove back. But I've always been so prone to fear and anxiety, and once an idea planted itself inside my neurotic little brain it was extremely difficult to scoop out. So I sat on the porch and listened to the rain and thought about Keith. I wondered what he would've been like if he made it past sixteen. If we'd still be friends and if he would have lived with me and Oz? Or would I have failed him in some other monumental way? Would he have drifted out of my life like everybody else I'd left behind in Scranton?

The rain was splashing me wet by this point, but I didn't go inside even when my phone started ringing.

"I need you to meet me at Brillobox." It was Noah.

"Why?"

"I just need you to do it, ok?"

I was practically soaked now.

"Is this about Junie? Because if it is, I've really had it and I have a lot of shit to deal with right—"

"Michael. Please."

The tone in his voice was so pleading that I couldn't say no. Noah needed me right that second and was only a five minute drive across town, and I so wanted to be of use to someone, anyone.

"Ok," I said. "I'll be there."

Before I left, I walked around the side of the house to the garage in the back. Oz's car. I bent over and grabbed the wet garage door handle. I made up my mind that if his car was still there, I'd call the police immediately, tell them my roommate hadn't been seen in a week, that his students hadn't seen him either, that he was missing and most likely depressed. But if it was gone, if Oz had indeed chosen to jump in his Cavalier and escape, then I would wait. I would give us both a little more time to buy into my fantasy, that Oz was traveling and not dead, that Oz had embarked on the great dusty highways to find solace, that he would return to us fixed and safe. I threw open the door. His car was gone.

The Brillobox, the hippest bar in Pittsburgh, was named after the Andy Warhol sculpture. It hosted vegan potlucks and dance parties in the attic complete with early-80s rap and world music. Flat screen televisions hung from the walls and the bartenders played a continuous loop of ironic films. Have you ever wanted to enjoy an overpriced pitcher of Yuengling while watching the Japanese cut of *Godzilla vs. Mothra*? Have you ever wanted to grind against a young photography major dressed like your grandmother while leotard clad homosexuals paint the walls full of unicorns? Then have I got a bar for you.

My friends hated it on the pretense that it was *too* hip, but Sloan—who'd grown up here in the city—nostalgically enjoyed it and sometimes had a hankering for their feta eggplant subs. I hoped this was the reason Noah had called me over, that he wanted to once again use me as a conversational buffer between himself and his chatty fiancé. But no such luck. Noah sat texting alone at the bar, an empty glass and bag of takeout in front of him.

"I bought a sub for Sloan and some spinach hummus and pita for you."

I ordered a Yuengling. "Yeah. Why?"

"I need you to bring this to her. Say we met up for a Sunday beer and I got called into Digital to code some last minute proofs."

"Oz got an F on one of his papers and disappeared."

"Dude. Look. I love Oz, but I can't really deal with his issues right now. I'm sure he just went home or something. I kind of have my own stuff."

The bartender poured me a beer. He wore a torn black shirt and we could see his curly bush of chest hair. I glared at him until he left us alone and kept my voice low. "Are you really that selfish? Oz needs us and all you can think about is some skank?"

"She's not a skank. And you don't know that's where I'm going."

"Where are you going?"

He slid the bag of food my way and laid a twenty on the bar. "Ok, fine. But Oz probably just needs to blow off steam. It'll do him good. Guy hasn't gotten laid in years. He'll be back in a month."

"In my experience these things can go pretty badly."

"Well, whatever. I gotta get out of here."

He stood to go, but I grabbed him by the shoulder. Something had come over me. The reappearance of Elaine, the disappearance of Oz. I could feel this fun and inconsequential world we'd built up since college falling into disrepair. I had to make one last stab to salvage the status quo, to insulate myself from eternal loneliness. "Do you love Sloan?"

"Despite what you might think, Michael, I'm still a good guy. I'm not a bad person."

It was just the two of us now. The bartender had slinked off to the back room. I let go of Noah's shoulder.

"I do love her. She's so intelligent and generous, and I know I don't love Junie. But the idea of only being with Sloan for the rest of my life..." He trailed off. "I'm just trying to figure out what I want. Junie's helping me with that. Maybe this is just a last fling, you know?"

My hands were trembling. I hadn't come to Brillobox with this confrontation in mind, but it all seemed connected in a way. How I had mocked Ivy's faith. How I had stood by while Noah cheated on Sloan. How I'd become so absorbed in my own drama that I hadn't even noticed Oz falling apart. How I had allowed Keith to die. They were all part of the same thing. Cowardice. Weakness. Inaction. It had to end. "I don't feel comfortable with this anymore. You need to figure out what you want and tell Sloan the truth," I said.

"Fuck. Give me a few days. But first, will you just bring this to her please? I have to at least talk with Junie."

I accepted his bag of takeout, its bottom soggy with grease. "I'm here for you," I said, and I wanted it to be true. I wanted to be there for Oz and Sloan and Noah and Ivy.

I wanted to be there for Keith.

Across town, Sloan answered her apartment door, her mouth a tight little line. "Where is he?"

"Oh. Noah? He got called into Digital."

"On a Sunday? Doing what?" She held the door inches from her face.

"A DVD emergency. Computer stuff. I'm just a subtitler. They don't tell me anything important. Bottom of the totem pole. Sub-basement of the totem pole really. I have to squint just to see that totem pole way up above me. It's like, 'Hello? Hello? Anybody listening up there at the top of that totem pole?'"

Sloan went inside and flung herself on the couch. I entered and hunted for silverware. The sink overflowed with dirty dishes and I had to settle for an opened bag of plastic forks behind a sack of rotting potatoes in the cupboard.

"Noah gave me money to grab us some food. What a guy, right?"

I took the armchair opposite Sloan and set the takeout bag on the coffee table. I pushed a stack of old *Paste* magazines aside to make room.

"Look, S. A feta eggplant sub! What wonder of wonders! What joy upon joys!"

"Can you *for once* be quiet?"

She stood and poured herself a glass of red wine. Then she disappeared into the bedroom. I didn't know if it was rude to eat without her, but Noah had ordered my hummus almost an hour ago and I was pretty sure hummus was one of those exotic food items that could go bad very quickly and kill you with angry bacteria. So I started to eat.

She emerged a moment later from the bedroom—her wine glass noticeably empty—and walked over to her webcam. She still wouldn't look at me. I loaded my mouth full of hummus and listened to her recite numbers into the void of the internet for an entire hour. "243,088. 243,089. 243,090." It sounded like the incantation of a nightmare. It sounded like the bedtime lullaby for a demographic doomed.

♠

I didn't get home until after midnight. My hair was disheveled, my stomach ached, and my mind had been reduced to protoplasm after an hour of listening to Sloan Smith count. I was in no position to be checking e-mail. I should've collapsed in my bed and fallen asleep to the familiar sounds of trains howling past the city, but I just couldn't resist peeking at gmail once before bed. Waiting for me was an electronic musing from Ivy Chase. The subject line read "Making Sense of Things" and boy, how badly I wanted to do that.

---

hide details

from:	**Ivy Chase** <IChase@gmail.com>	April 19 (3 hours ago)
to:	Michael Bishop <FartGod69XXX@gmail.com>	
subject:	Making Sense of Things	
mailed-by	gmail.com	

Dear Michael,

This is a hard e-mail to write, so I'm just going to come out and say the things that need said. I've been having a hard time with

160

everything that's going on between us and your completely irrational reaction to my spirituality. So I went to the only real friend I have here in town for advice, Elaine. She didn't give me the details, so you don't have to worry, but she told me how religious you used to be and about what happened to her brother.

I understand why you've never told me you were best friends with him, but I want to let you know I understand loss, and I would love it if you told me your story. Michael, I care about you. We both have this really awful thing in common. Keith's death. Danielle's death. And I just want to talk to you. Maybe we can make sense of it together. I think we can fix each other.

-Ivy

I reread that e-mail three times. Then I guzzled a bottle of Yuengling and stifled my impulse to pace. Where did she get off claiming she could fix me? Oh, and by the way, thanks for keeping quiet about the whole Keith thing, Elaine.

But then, after the initial shock and rage wore off, I began to consider Ivy's e-mail in a different, kinder light. In many ways, weren't the contents of Ivy's message something I'd longed to hear since high school? What I'd wanted Sloan or Oz or anyone to say, that they understood I'd gone through something significant and traumatic, that they could fix me and make me feel more like a genuine person?

I zipped up an old windbreaker and hopped in my Saturn. I sped across the highway and called Ivy when I reached Dormont, told her to wait outside her house. She was sitting on the stoop when I pulled up, her feet dangling below in flip flops. The house lights were off and she wore only a cotton slip. I checked my watch. It was almost two in the morning. In seven hours I'd have to be at my desk at Digital Deluxe downloading the latest batch of un-proofed featurettes. I leaned over the shifter and unlocked the passenger door.

"It's late." She shut it behind her.

Her hair stuck flat to one side of her head. I was sweating and flipped on the AC. All of Dormont had gone dark and the only noise came from the engine pumping artificial air into our mouths and bodies and lungs and hearts. I took Ivy's hands in mine. I hadn't told Noah or Sloan or Oz. I'd structured the last seven years of my life around ignoring the past. I looked into Ivy's eyes and wondered if I was taking my first true step into adulthood, my Neil Armstrongs spurred on by Oz's disappearance and a desire to make things right.

I told her about Keith Tedesco. And that singular event required so much exposition that I found myself dovetailing back in time, explaining the incident on Route 6, my years glued in front of the Nintendo Entertainment System, how Keith and I only managed to survive St. Anthony's together, my crush on Elaine, the way Keith dumped Annie and finally came out of the closet, his suicide, his suicide, his suicide.

"I found out on family vacation. The opposite of you. Your friend Danielle died in the ocean. I waded out into the ocean after I found out. I still feel so guilty. If only I hadn't been such a fundamentalist nut job I could have saved him. He couldn't deal with the idea of facing high school, not to mention his coming out, alone. That's on me. No matter what I do, I can't go back and fix things. He's gone."

She held me against her chest. "It's ok to feel this way, Michael, but you shouldn't blame yourself. I felt the same way when Danielle died, and there was absolutely nothing I could have done about it. Why don't you talk to Elaine about this? You need resolution. You need to put this behind you even if it's always a part of who you are. What about Keith's mother? Have you tried talking to her?"

I listened to Ivy's heartbeat, a steady drum that seemed to contain every answer in this unknowable world. "I've really wanted to talk to Mrs. Tedesco over the years, but I'm nervous. Something my mom told me about the wake. We went through the line in the funeral parlor, and when my mom hugged Mrs. T she asked how she was. She said she was doing as well as could be expected, that she was taking some pills prescribed to her by her doctor, that maybe she'd need to howl at the moon every once in awhile but she hoped that wouldn't be held against her." I looked up into Ivy's eyes. "I know Mrs. Tedesco hasn't turned into some gargoyle. She still has Elaine after all. But I just can't bring myself to go to her house, Keith's old house, and really atone for everything I've done. That image of her howling at the moon... It's just too much."

"You need to do it, Michael. I'm sure she'd love to hear from you, and it's the only way forward. Just be honest and you'll feel so much better when it's over. Why don't you start with Elaine? A warm up?"

"I know," I said. "All right, I'll talk with Elaine first. I promise."

She wrapped her arms around me and nuzzled her face against my chest. "You know, it's funny. We're different on so many levels, you and I. But this tragedy connects us. I know what you've gone through, what you're still going through. Keith's death wasn't your fault." She squeezed my hands. "Being with someone like you, this is how I always imagined my life."

I held her closer. I kissed her hair, her forehead, each of her salty eyelids. I kissed her neck and slowly made my way to that sweet spot beneath her ear. "I love you," I whispered. She told me her parents were out-of-town at a faith conference in Lancaster. She wanted to know if I'd come inside, if I'd spend the night.

Inside, we were tender and loving and totally amazing, and afterwards I spooned her and faced the open window. The sun was rising in the east, washing everything clean with its grace. I fell asleep with my face buried in Ivy's blonde hair.

I remember thinking I could still be saved, that I could still become a better version of myself even after everything that had gone so very, very wrong.

The alarm went off at seven. I scratched my stubble and studied the peaks and dips of Ivy's sleeping body. She would never hurt a soul, didn't have it in her. She was infinitely decent and possessed true blue qualities I'd been searching for my entire life. Was it possible to transform myself into an all-new, all-different Michael Bishop, one deserving of Ivy and the sweet adoration of this entire world?

In the shower, I hummed along to old Monkees songs. Then I took a nice, leisurely shave using Mr. Chase's Old Spice and one of Mrs. Chase's disposables. My choice of dress was lacking—yesterday's Lacoste and khakis—but I wasn't about to let a thing like that get me down. I had a decent job, I lived in a kickass city, I had the perfect girlfriend, and most of all, I was alive!

Ivy stood in the kitchen over the stove. The entire downstairs smelled of sugar and cinnamon.

"Darling?"

"Michael."

I came up behind her and kissed her on the cheek, then tapped her twice on that plentiful behind, that gregarious booty that gave me an erection just by brushing against it. She was cooking French toast. And bacon! And scrambled eggs! She even used powdered sugar and ground cinnamon. I longed for a newspaper. I wanted to peruse the business section and murmur "Mmm" and "Hmm" at the indecipherable jumble of stock numbers. I wanted to fix myself some sherry and smoke a Cuban. It took everything I had not to lick the plate clean, drop to my knees, and hug Ivy's ankles till the rapidly approaching end of time.

Later, Ivy bid me adieu from the doorway. Her hair was the color of butter under the early morning sun. She gave me a vigorous wave and I grinned like an idiot and thought about beagles and clouds and ice cream.

I arrived at Digital Deluxe ten minutes early and found a miraculous parking space only three blocks away. By ten, I completed seven featurettes for *P.S. I Love You* and two episodes of *Two and a Half Men: The Third Season*. By lunch, I finished the entire *American Idol Season Six Finale*. I was sweating by early afternoon and only took a break to scan Facebook once.

Ivy Chase is truly, utterly happy.

Other than this brief interlude, I focused one-hundred percent on my subtitling duties. At least until a meaty claw gripped down on my shoulder.

It was Hudelson. He tapped out a little song on my shoulder. "Got a message from Madhuri today, Bishop. Said you're doing the work of two men." He kicked at my shins. "You hiding somebody down there? You hire an illegal immigrant?"

"No, sir. No illegal immigrants. Just me."

He nodded. "That's fine as frog hair, son. Fine as goddamn frog hair. That's what we like to see here at Digital Deluxe. Initiative."

"Yes sir."

"You know, I was talking to some of my supervisors today and we were discussing various possibilities if we canned the subtitling division here in Pittsburgh. Do you know what they're thinking? Compression Error."

I'd heard rumors of the impending arrival of Compression Error from Noah and some of the IT boys. Compression Error involved sitting in a mini movie theatre and watching the same DVD over and over again on slow while scanning the screen for dead pixels. First with the English audio track, then with the Spanish, the Director's Commentary, and so on and so forth until an entire week was lost to the same ninety minutes of Bill Murray's tragicomedy *Garfield*.

"Oh, wow," I said. "Compression Error."

"Compression Error! How about that, Michael? If this subtitling venture goes all Titanic on us, would you like to be considered for a spot on our Compression Error Team?"

"Oh, that sounds like something I'd definitely be interested in possibly considering, Mr. Hudelson."

Work was great and life was great. Ivy practically moved in with me after the Keith revelation citing Sloan's need for wedding help to her parents. I came home each and every day to find her at my computer, surfing Facebook, using InDesign to create more propaganda for her father's church—that was just temporary, she assured me, soon she would branch out and get real PR work. And Ivy's ambition rekindled my own. The two of us spent many a night back to back: Ivy testing out fonts while I labored over my world of wacky robot human hybrids. We pretended we lived in my apartment year round, that we had kids, had real lives together.

But whenever Ivy went home to visit her parents or hang out with Elaine, I'd sneak inside Oz's dusty room and sit on his bed. I didn't turn on the lights. I didn't open the windows. I booted up his MacBook and logged onto Keith Tedesco's Facebook profile.

Keith Tedesco is content after speaking with his good friend who he would never let down, Owen Osborne III. Oz is totally safe and fine. Nothing bad is going to happen. He didn't kill himself. No one else is going to die.

I shut down the computer. I sat in the darkness. I had no clue that very soon I would lose everyone I cared about.

When My Life Imploded

I stood outside the entrance to Phipps, the university greenhouse shaped like a glass turtle, and squinted for the familiar outline of Elaine Tedesco inside. I spotted her through the window sipping coffee in the café. She'd texted me earlier saying she wanted to speak with me, that I'd put off this meeting for far too long, and this time I obliged because of Ivy's insistence. I had promised her after all. I rubbed my sweaty palms against the back of my pants and entered the eerily tropical air of the Phipps Conservatory.

Instrumental jazz renditions of late-90s love songs pumped in overhead. I touched Elaine on the shoulder and flashed her The Most Confident Grin in the Universe. "The Phipps Conservatory? Really?" I asked.

"I like it here. I like the exhibits. There's a new one by

some German welder and I thought I could kill two birds with one stone."

"You want to walk through?"

"Sure."

So we walked. Up the stairs that led to the greenhouse proper and into that lush, sweaty world of plants! Phipps is laid out like a maze, and I was surprised by how pleasant it was to stroll through its moist architecture pausing only to observe a massive pink flower or the horrific metallic creatures artist Arthur Machler had erected and hidden within the flora.

We stopped at an aquarium. Elaine pressed a red button on its base. A light buzzed to life beneath the waters revealing dozens and dozens of orange and white fish recalling the dead koi from the Chases' pond. The glowing waters cast strange waves of light across our faces. I knelt down and pressed my hand to the glass. A fish blinked at me. The smell reminded me of the YMCA.

"So I guess you know what this is about, right?" Elaine asked. "I want to talk about Keith."

"Let's not do it here though. I don't want to have this conversation in front of the fish."

We left the aquarium and entered a dark hallway, its walls covered in vines, a copper robot standing sentry in the center. I touched its arm even though you weren't really supposed to. It was built in rectangles, humanoid in structure, two roses standing in for eyeballs.

Elaine sat on a bench by the robot. "Keith's loss was very hard on all of us. But it was really obvious to me when I arrived that you hadn't told a single one of your friends about him."

"I told Ivy," I snapped. "Eventually."

She softened. She opened her purse and produced a pack of gum. She offered me a stick and I accepted.

"You told Ivy after I made it necessary. I just don't think you've dealt with his… death."

She didn't say suicide, but that slight hesitation, the momentary pause was all I needed to see the truth: that I was not alone in the knowledge—or at the very least, the strong suspicion—that Keith's death was no accident, but a regrettable and preventable suicide.

"How do you 'deal with it', Elaine? The Synoptic Gospels?"

"Yes. It gives me peace of mind. What's so bad about that?"

"Ok. But why do you even care if I've dealt with it? We were never that good of friends and I haven't even seen you since Bishop O'Hara."

"It's my mother," Elaine said after a pause. "She always asks about you, how you're doing, what your life's like, and at first I thought it was ok, that it was natural to be curious about the life your dead son's best friend ends up having. Because, you know, that's the closest thing to knowing what would have happened to Keith if he'd lived. Watching you, I mean."

I nodded. I was the dead boy's stand-in.

"And my mother, well she's a saint," Elaine continued. "Strongest woman I've ever met. And she really has moved on with her life. She really has. But I think it hurts her that you haven't gone to visit her since the funeral. We all know you've been avoiding her."

"I didn't mean to-"

"Nobody meant for any of this to happen."

A family entered the hall, two parents and a little girl between them. Her hair was pulled back in a ponytail and she wore a pink puffy jacket even though it was way too warm for it in this sauna of a conservatory. But she marched through the displays without a word of complaint, her dim-witted parents bopping along clueless to anyone outside their insular universe. Elaine and I watched them and said nothing till they passed.

"Look, I don't want to keep you." Elaine slid the straps of her purse over her shoulder. "I just think you should visit my mother. She would be so utterly appreciative of it, and Michael, honestly, I think it would do you a world of good. Just be honest with her, that's all I ask."

We hugged, and as she walked toward the exit I knew that no matter how much soul searching I did, I would never be as at home in the world as someone like Elaine Tedesco. I balled my trembling hands and called out to her.

"I haven't visited home in a really long time." I paused here to make sure this was what I wanted, that this was really what I needed. "Maybe I'll go pay a visit to your mother. Talk to her about Keith."

I thought she might rush over, wrap me in a bear hug, start crying, maybe even explain that she'd always loved me and regretted not giving me the time of day back in high school now that I was so totally, completely in love with the saintly Ivy Chase, but Elaine Tedesco just stood there and smiled. She gave a quick little wave and that was it, leaving me alone in the hallway to wonder if this was what it felt like to be a good person, if the only reward for kindness was the unmistakable emotion I felt in the dampness of the greenhouse: happiness.

Those feelings of happiness were unfortunately short-lived, as my life imploded the very next day. It began like any other Friday. My assignments at work weren't particularly difficult as I'd been given an endless array of *Loony Tunes* episodes for the DVD rereleases, and obviously, there's not a lot of dialogue to correct in Road Runner cartoons. And it was while typing "Meep Meep" for what felt like the millionth time when I noticed Mr. Hudelson coming straight toward me.

"Michael."

I tugged off my headphones. My first ill-fated thought upon seeing Hudelson was that he'd come to deliver a promotion.

"I would like it very much if you would accompany me to the roof, Michael."

I never knew that Mr. Hudelson, or anyone from Digital Deluxe for that matter, had access to the roof, but that didn't deter me from following him into the elevator. It deposited us on the tenth floor where there was only one other office, some nebulous operation called Triton Rubber Bands. It suddenly seemed significant that I'd worked unknowingly beneath rubber band salesmen for the last thousand-plus days of my life, but I couldn't pinpoint why.

The roof was covered with gravel and coiled exhaust pipes that spewed puffs of smog. Hudelson walked to the far edge—his loafers crunching beneath him, his tie flapping in the wind—where all of East Carson looked flattened against the skyline and three converging rivers, those endless yellow bridges. We stood side-by-side as Hudelson shook his head.

"Being Operations Manager of a Digital Deluxe Branch is pretty taxing, Michael. That's why I like to come up here when I get stressed. Just to relax and think about this great city of ours. Then everything inside doesn't seem so bad or so big. Do you understand that, Michael? Can you see what I'm driving at?"

"Sure." I imagined Bentleys and Ferraris, private jets and stretch limousines with aquariums inside. Golden hover motorcycles powered by smiles.

"That's why I wanted you to see this. We've had an interesting roller coaster ride of a relationship, haven't we? What with the Tyler Perry business and all. But I want you to know that TP doesn't have anything to do with this decision."

"Sir?"

"I got the orders today. They're dismantling our subtitling division. And they're not putting together the Compression Error team until later this year. But they have offered you your same job over in Bangladesh."

Bangladesh?

Bangladesh?

For real, for real?

What surprised me was how quickly I made my decision. I've always been a highly indecisive creature plagued by neuroses and a fear of change and the future, and I always imagined that if presented with a life altering decision, that I would require hours, days, potentially months to come to an even then floundering conclusion. That was not the case. I studied the familiar Pittsburgh skyline and knew that I could not, would not leave. Even in spite of my friends' various crises, I still had Ivy. I still had Ivy!

"I'm sorry. I don't think I'm going to be able to do that."

"Well that's a shame, Michael. Because now I have to fire you."

I stood there next to Mr. Hudelson and watched a red incline car climb out of the decadence of Station Square—home to the Hard Rock Café and Matrix Dance Lounge—and into the affluent neighborhood up over the mountains. It moved so slowly and I wondered if anyone still used inclines as a legitimate form of transportation, or if they were akin to a unicycle or row boat: ironic vehicles. As for my sudden termination from the ranks of Digital Deluxe? I was in shock. I was numb.

"You can finish out the day if you prefer," Hudelson said. "Clean out your desk, whatever."

I loosened my tie. I thought about my Dilbert calendar. "I think I'll just go home. Can you not tell anyone till Monday? I don't want any flowery goodbyes."

"You're all right, kid." He stuck out his paw and I shook

it. What else was there to do? How could I feel any malice for this small man? I was sure he had no hand in my destruction, and like myself, existed only as a tiny cog in the vast machinations of Digital Deluxe and its many, many parent corporations. And what was the fate of one man to Disney, Time Warner, Newscorp, the maleficent entities of Oz's "late-era capitalism" that had driven him to the open roads of America, or even worse, death?

Hudelson rode the elevator with me to the third floor where I continued on without him to the ground level. And just like that, I was expelled into the looming recession and the wilds of the Pittsburgh unemployed. The street smelled of boiled peanuts and yams.

I rode the bus home through the undergraduate section of town. I'd commuted through there every day for years, but now I didn't have some book to bury my nose in—I'd forgotten the Welles bio in my desk. I watched throngs of students file out of the Cathedral of Learning. I saw bikini clad co-eds tanning and playing Frisbee in the park next to the library. I looked on in longing as we passed the street where Oz and I once lived in a tenement. It wasn't until the bus drove through the university that the full weight of my termination hit me, and in a moment of unparalleled cartoony gesturing, I wrung my hands like a creeper straight out of Poe. I had savings tucked away—two-thousand dollars untouched from my graduation party—and whatever menial monies I could con from the unemployment barons. But that wouldn't last in this economy. That wouldn't support the lavish lifestyle Ivy and I had begun to enjoy: overpriced octopi for dinner, omelets from Pamela's for breakfast, fifty dollar checks at the Cage so we could get drunk, be jolly and have Important Talks About The Future And The Nature Of Fate.

I missed my stop. I got off two blocks out of my way and walked back uphill to my apartment where Ivy would be waiting. What could I possibly say to her? I'd never brought up my job troubles before and now I had to blindside her with this? And Hudelson! Fucking Hudelson! Like a self-centered teenager, my fear and self-loathing turned itself on everyone within striking distance. It was Hudelson's fault! And Tyler Perry! Those guys had been out to get me from the beginning. Didn't anyone have a brother's back anymore?

Fuck you, Tyler Perry!

My armpits were soaked by the time I walked inside. I could hear Ivy in the shower and didn't want to scare her—she was the only one here during the afternoons—so I tiptoed past her and into the bedroom. The room was dark except for the glowing computer screen, and could anyone really blame me for pausing in front of it to have myself a little looksie? Haven't we as a people been trained through years of exposure to screen culture—televisions, computers, movies, GameBoys, cell phones, iPods, etc. etc.—to stop and take notice of the defining object of this ominous century? She'd left up Facebook, the private message section. I leaned in close and read the name of the person she'd been chatting with for what appeared to be quite some time. Tommy Mendocino, the carpenter from New York City. I glanced over my shoulder to the bathroom. Ivy was still showering unaware of my presence, so I shut the door quietly and sat down to read.

💬 Clarifications
Between <u>Tommy Mendocino</u> and <u>Ivy Chase</u>

Tommy Mendocino   February 22 at 9:33pm
I,

I know things got heated last week, but I wanted to apologize. I said some things I shouldn't have, and I guess I just wasn't expecting the break up. But I wanted you to know that regardless of what happens between us in the future, I will always respect you. You are a wonderful person and as long as you keep Christ in your heart you will never go down a bad path.

I see through Facebook that you have a new boyfriend. Things make more sense now, and I just hope he can nourish you spiritually, Ivy, because no matter what you think may have changed during college, you will always be, first and foremost, a Christian woman.

If you ever want to talk, you know I'm here for you.

Always,
T

Ivy Chase   February 23 at 11:19am
Tommy,

Thanks for the kind words. I'm sure our paths will cross again.

-Ivy

Tommy Mendocino   March 14 at 4:15pm
I,

I know how much you adored Father Scuderi, and he delivered an excellent sermon this week. I've linked to the podcast. Check it out and let me know what you think. I'm especially interested in your opinions on his "paradox of inter-faith coupling in the modern era."

Always,
T

Ivy Chase   March 15 at 10:46pm

Tommy,

Listened to the podcast. Interesting stuff there. Would
definitely agree that inter-faith relationships are more difficult
to maintain than a couple who has the same opinions on faith,
but aren't the really good things in life worth fighting for? Look,
I know you sent this because you probably stalked Michael's
profile and saw that under Religion he put "Irony/Hot Dogs,"
but he really is a good guy. We don't talk about spirituality. It
doesn't even come up.

-Ivy

Ivy Chase   April 14 at 1:45pm

Tommy,

Hi. I know it's been awhile, and you've probably got a ton on
your plate. But I really need someone to talk to with values
similar to mine.

Listen, I know this is weird. But I've been having problems with
Michael. He's agnostic at best. He came to one of my dad's
services and was horrified. He freaked out. We haven't really
spoken in a few days, and oh my God, yes I know how weird it
is to discuss this with you of all people, but I didn't know who
else to turn to. You had a lot of girlfriends before me. Were any
of them secular? Did it lead to a lot of problems?

Oh, I ran across a book of poetry I think you'd really like. *All of
Us* by Raymond Carver who I know you love. Check it out.

-Ivy

Tommy Mendocino   April 15 at 6:22pm

I,

I'm really glad you messaged me. You could have called. It's weird to talk to each other over screens, don't you think?

Secular significant others. I can understand your attraction because that's definitely a stage I went through. Opposites attract right? But what you're going to find out is that those people can't nourish you spiritually. And although that might be fine for some people, it's not fine for you, Ivy Chase. I know you too well. Don't you want to raise your children in the church? If this beau of yours "freaked out" over a single service of your father's, then how do you think he'd feel about his children being baptized, confirmed, and so on and so forth? Think of all the hours we spent in my apartment drinking tea and talking about God and the world. Could you go without that your whole life? I couldn't.

I read the Carver. I particularly liked the bit about feeling beloved in "Late Fragment."

Ivy. I miss you. Do you miss me?

Always,

T

Ivy Chase   May 3 at 3:06pm

Tommy,

Thanks for the phone call last night. You know you'll always have a special place in my heart, and you know I miss you dearly. But Michael's like a lost puppy and I think that I can make him come back around.

I think I can return him to the fold.

-Ivy

Tommy Mendocino   May 3 at 7:41pm

I,

What you're describing doesn't really sound like a boyfriend,
it sounds like one of your community service projects. So I've
only got one question for you, Ives. Do you love him?

Always,

T

Do you love him? I sat there listening to Ivy finish up in
the shower, then brush her teeth. *Do you love him?* And she'd
been talking to her ex-boyfriend all this time getting something she could never get from me: *spiritual nourishment.*

The bathroom door slapped opened. The hallway filled
with steam. Ivy appeared in the doorway with a towel
wrapped around her torso and a second one over her blonde
hair. She was absentmindedly drying it when she saw me,
stopped and screamed.

I didn't move to comfort her. I stayed right there in the
chair and stared.

"Michael! What are you doing home?"

I'm not going to lie and say her half-nakedness didn't give
me a surge of power. My emotions were all over the place:
oblivion one minute, rage the next. I felt like I might spontaneously combust and only wanted to trap Ivy within the
blast radius.

"I got fired."

Her face dropped and she rushed forward with intent to
hug. But I held her at arm's length. I pointed to the glowing
computer screen. "What's this?"

Her eyebrows narrowed. "Are you reading my messages?"

"You left them up on *my* computer."

"That's not the point. You're never home at this time.
Those are private."

She opened the bottom drawer of my dresser where she kept her things. She slid on a pair of cotton underwear, then a night shirt that came down to her thighs. I fetishized that shirt even more than her lacey things because of its absolute intimacy.

"Did you read them?" she asked.

"Read what?"

"I saw his picture up there. I know whose messages you were looking at."

"Yeah. I read them." My voice was sharp. I wanted Ivy to feel this. "How long have you been talking with him on the phone?"

She sat on the floor and hugged her knees close to her chest. "Just since last month. After you came to my dad's service."

"Do you love me?"

The fan blades overhead. A car honked outside. Ivy pulled her hair into a ponytail. She stood up and looked like she wanted to touch me, hold me, but she didn't.

"I care about you, Michael. You can't spend this much time with someone and not care about them."

"But you don't love me."

Her face said it all. I tried not to dwell on the little things I would miss, all those secret jokes, all those private memories. I could already feel them evaporating, was already cognizant of the end Sloan had predicted so long ago over sandwiches at the Double Wide.

Ivy lowered her eyes, refused to look at me. "No. It's not a love for the ages I guess."

"Do you love him?" I asked. "Tommy?"

"I don't know." Her eyes pleaded for me to stop. "Maybe. I might."

Hearing those words, knowing what they meant, that we were fast approaching the end… it felt a little like dying. I had begun, only just begun, to tentatively imagine a future for

Ivy and me. How I would rise through the ranks of Digital Deluxe only until my comic took off and saw print, maybe a multi-million dollar movie deal starring Tobey Maguire and Christian Bale. Then we'd get married and move, maybe to New York? London? Paris? Wherever the hell we wanted. We could have kids. They would look like Ivy, and everything would be completely beautiful and nothing would ever go wrong again. But now, it was obvious that this phantom life would go unlived. I imagined this was how people who die young must feel in their final moments, picturing what might have been, realizing that everything they thought was theirs had slipped through their fingers. I thought of Keith and Danielle, that parallel loss, how even that shared burden could not hold us together.

"I think you should leave," I said.

She did not cry, did not make a scene. She packed a bag with her belongings and left without another word, just a tender squeeze of my shoulder that for a second seemed to mean so much more than it ever really could.

So I did what any other reasonable twenty-something would do in the early days of the 21st century. I drove to the liquor store and purchased two great handles of Crown Royal. Then I stopped at the deli and picked up two cases of Yuengling. I returned home and sprawled out on the hardwood floor, occasionally standing up to bellow at the heavens or impotently punch the wall with my femme fist. I drank whiskey straight from the bottle and took breaks with my good friend Dr. Yuengling. I kept a bag of garlic croutons at my side and occasionally reached in for a handful to munch on. I thought about Ivy, Ivy, Ivy, but I spent even more time imagining Oz and what might have happened to him. Maybe he was out west somewhere spending his days in a bright hotel pool charming beautiful woman after beautiful woman. And maybe he was already dead. I knew time was running out for both of us, that I'd waited far too long for some sign of encouragement that might never come. I became drunker and drunker and wanted so badly for him to be with me, for Oz to listen to my problems and tell me that everything was going to be ok.

Around drink number seven, I received a phone call. I cleared my throat and ironically took the tone of an early-nineties gangsta rapper. "Who the fuck this be?"

"Michael?"

"Yo." I loudly chewed croutons.

"Are you drunk?"

"Who this be?"

"Sloan."

Ah, Sloan Smith! I paid special attention to the tone of her voice. It didn't sound particularly patronizing and I attributed this to that goon Hudelson actually keeping his word and not telling people I'd been shit-canned.

"Michael. Is Noah with you? He never came home after work and he's not picking up his cell. I thought maybe he'd be with you."

What was abundantly obvious was that Noah had not heeded my earlier Brillobox request. He had not told Sloan the truth and was, most likely, out knocking boots with Junie Censulla that very second. Suddenly everything became clear to me. My job was gone. Ivy was gone. Oz was gone. Keith was gone. And I had put off being honest with Sloan for far too long. I resealed my bag of croutons and yelled into the phone. "I'll meet you at the bar by your apartment in ten minutes. Be there!"

I slugged back the whiskey and stumbled out to my car, imagining myself ascending to Godzilla-like proportions, using my atomic breath to blow everything terrible about this dumb fucking generation to dust.

I knew I shouldn't drive. And I'm not one of those guys who drinks and drives like it ain't no thang. I remembered that white van on Route 6 and drove twenty miles per hour calling on the well of experience I'd accrued during marathon sessions of racing games for Nintendo. I parked and entered the bar, eager to find Sloan and get this over with. Kelly's was cramped and dank, filled with people in newsboy hats and boas, the walls blood red, a nightmare version of the Squirrel Cage. I found Sloan in a vinyl booth and slid in across from her. She sipped a vodka something. She fiddled with her purse and produced a box of Lucky Strikes along with a cheap Bic lighter.

"You smoking again?"

"In situations of extreme duress."

The waitress came over and took my drink order. She was mannish with a cropped haircut and plain button down shirt. I looked her square in the eye and demanded a whiskey neat.

"Is liquor really a good decision right now?" Sloan asked.

"What's that supposed to mean?"

"You're slurring. Did you drive here?"

"Maybe."

She took off her glasses and hid them in her purse with her cigs and lighter and god knew what other secret talismans. The waitress returned with my whiskey.

"So what is it this time? Noah have to work late again on a Friday night?"

I had come to denounce the actions of Noah Black and reveal to Sloan Smith once and for all that she had been cheated on and that I was complicit. But now that I had arrived and the moment for action was here, I froze. Performance anxiety. Womp womp.

"When did you become Noah's messenger boy anyway?" Sloan asked. "I know you've always had this sad little big brother deal, but Jesus, Michael, show some self-respect. Shouldn't you be out with Ivy praying or something?"

I finished the whiskey in a series of long gulps. "When did you become so cold?"

She killed the vodka and signaled the waitress for two more drinks. Hipsters in the booth behind us discussed the recent *Iron Man* movie. They thought it promoted a pro-Bush agenda. I wanted to scream and tell those jerks they didn't know a goddamned thing about alcoholic genius Tony Stark, the man responsible for the death of his best friend Captain America, the World War II Super Solider.

Sloan took another drag and aimed her cigarette at the Iron Man convo. "It ever bother you, Michael, that our generation has yet to produce a great work of art? That all we've managed to do is regurgitate pop culture on YouTube and Facebook and Twitter?"

"No. Never."

"I figured. When we first met, I thought you'd go onto do something really great, really important. And I just wanted to be there when it happened. But you're not the type. You're more critic than artist. Always have been. Too obsessed with minutiae. No interest in the big picture."

"I have interest in pictures."

"I'm sure you do, just like Oz. And where is he now?" She sipped her vodka, her eyes full of mourning. "What happened to us? We all had so much promise."

"I lost my job," I told her. "Me and Ivy are done."

"Well, I don't want to say I told you so, but I told you so. She's a sheep in wolves' clothing. You think she's your typical, ironic modern girl, but she's not."

"Yeah?" I downed the second whiskey. "And what about you? Little miss art student who counts on the internet. What about you and Noah? How's that going exactly?"

"Noah has extreme intimacy issues and a fear of commitment. Like most men, he doesn't like himself very much and projects it outwards. Thinks if he gains some type of stature it'll make up for all his perceived shortcomings." She stubbed out her Lucky Strike and lit another. "You think I don't know he's cheating on me? You all must think I'm some kind of fucking idiot, huh?"

"I was going to tell you. How long did you know?"

"Awhile. Just had a feeling."

"So why are you still with him? Why'd you say yes when he proposed?"

"I couldn't tell you why I've done a single thing in my entire life." She shook the ash free from her cig. "Let's do shots."

We abandoned the booth and took up shop at the bar, because if you have a mind to get seriously hammered you're not going to do it in a booth. Takes too long. You sit at the bar and if you've got the cash, you can get a fresh drink every few minutes if you're gregarious or moderately handsome. And Michael Bishop is nothing if not gregarious and moderately handsome.

"Two shots of your fugliest whiskey, please," I announced.

The bartender returned with two glasses of Yukon Jack, the self-proclaimed Black Sheep of Canadian Whiskey. I felt like I'd slipped back in time to my college years, those wonderful/terrible days spent roaming the undergraduate ghetto in a stupor.

"What are you going to do about Noah?" I asked.

"I think I'm going to end it. This is all just too much." She swirled her glass. "What are you going to do about Oz?"

"I don't know. What do you think I should do?"

"Track him down or tell somebody who can."

I nodded. We drank more. The bartender shouted last call and we wandered outside, our faces sweaty, slippery, infinite, the world tilting out of control.

"Well S., peace bitches." I pointed toward my car.

She pulled me by the waist and pointed in the opposite

direction. "Rummage House's that way, friend. I'm not letting you drive. You're destroyed."

I didn't need much convincing. All I had to remember was my nonexistent job, the termination of my relationship with Ivy, and of course, the empty bedroom across from my own, Oz. I still wanted desperately to believe that he was out there somewhere getting his bearings straight, but it was becoming more and more difficult with each new day. He was potentially dead, and I had done nothing, learned nothing, Keith's ghost mocking us from beyond the eternal.

We staggered toward Sloan's apartment three blocks away. At the end of each block we took a well-deserved rest. She slung her arm around my hip, and at first, I thought she was mothering me, that she thought I was too drunk to continue without her guiding hand. To be honest this was probably true. But during our second end-of-the-block break, I noticed Sloan's head sagging to the side, that her feet weren't pointed straight but impossibly inward. Like she hadn't walked a day in her life.

"You know," Sloan said quickly, "that I used to have a major, stupid crush on you back in college?" She chuckled under her breath. "Oz loved me, and I loved you, and you had a love/hate relationship with yourself. What a triangle. You're so oblivious to the world around you that it's almost, *almost* endearing. But you're such an asshole. You know that, right? How terrible you are? Remember that time we slept together and you didn't even talk to me about it afterwards?" She paused here. "Don't worry. I don't feel that way anymore. I've outgrown pining over jerks. I've outgrown you."

I pulled her close. I needed so badly at that moment to be loved, to feel anything at all other than pain. I kissed her beneath the streetlight while she squeezed both my hands. At the end of the third block, just one away from Rummage House, we made out.

The forced march through her apartment building was

arduous and only made bearable thanks to a brief elevator ride in which Sloan pinned me against the wall and pushed her lips against mine, frenzied. We spilled out into the hallway, found her apartment, and didn't even make it to the bed. We collapsed on the floor and fumbled with our bodies and clothes over the hardwood. I was too drunk and produced something barely classifiable as a boner. It took a long time, and not even a single second came close to matching that long ago evening in her dorm room: effervescent with the knowledge that I was young, that the world owed me everything. I finished and rolled onto my back. The only sensation I felt was disgust, the absolute certainty that I had made yet another mistake, that I was backsliding. I pulled the slippery condom off with my thumb and index finger. I kept it at my side holstered like a weapon.

Sloan tugged on her underwear, reset her bra. I slid on my boxers, and together we sat on the floor, train whistles faint in the distance. A minute passed, enough time for our breathing to return to normal, before Sloan stood and reached for my condom-free hand. "I want you to do something for me."

She led me to the bench in front of her computer and turned on the webcam. I knew what was coming.

"Say it with me," she said. "249,993. 249,994. 249,995."

We counted all the way to the long-awaited 250,000. A six-month journey finally at its conclusion, the ultimate release. When it was over, Sloan turned off the webcam and stayed very still. She stared at the computer while I wondered what she'd become, what every person on the face of the earth was turning into, some new type of human indoctrinated by screens and microchips and nuclear/religious fallout. I knew what Oz thought about her counting project. I knew what Ivy thought. But never before had I been able to articulate my own feelings about it. Only then, sitting half-nude alongside her when it was finally over did I grasp its purpose. All the viewers she'd earned. It proved her thesis. That people could be entertained by anything, even something that was literally meaningless like hours of counting into a webcam.

"You think everything is pointless, don't you?" I asked.

"I don't know, Michael. Let's not assign a meaning to it, all right? I hate meanings." She touched my knee as she clicked into Facebook. "I'm really glad I finished it with you though."

"Did you ever tell Noah? About that night we slept together in college? Did you ever tell him how Oz felt?"

"No. But you know he's going to see this right? Noah? He's going to see us counting almost naked and put two and two together. You know Ivy will see it too."

"I know," I said. "I get it."

"Good." She put her arm around my shoulder. "Then it's probably best for you to go."

I dressed and lingered in her outside hallway. Sloan stood behind her barely open door. Here was that beautiful face that had been such a constant in my life these seven long years. What do you say to a person like that? What on earth could you possibly say?

"What are you going to do now?" I asked.

"I think I'm going to hide out at my mother's for awhile. I need a change of scenery."

"Will I see you again?" It felt corny. But it wasn't like Sloan and Noah and I were going to be sharing lunch at the Double Wide anytime soon. This was change at the fundamental level.

Her forehead scrunched and even in my sorry, drunken state I could tell she gave the question a lot of thought before answering. "I don't know, Michael. Let's just leave it at that. A question."

The Crimson and Gold
of a Brilliant Failure

The next morning I awoke to the noise of someone pruning a tree outside my window. I cradled my aching noggin
and peeked through the curtains. There, beyond the fence
next door, stood a man in flannel and jeans snipping off tree
branches one after another. I watched this hired gun of Squirrel Hill Lawn Care prune down tree after tree. How strange
it was in this post-Ivy, post-Sloan-and-Noah, post-post-post
world that there still existed people who cared about The
State of Their Yard and were rapidly preparing for the onset
of a summer I would now have to spend in isolation.

I logged onto Facebook. Overnight, Ivy had changed her
relationship status to single. Mine still said in a relationship,
but the link to Ivy's profile was gone. That's when everything
became real for me—the break-up, the finality of everything.
Not watching Ivy leave with her things, not sleeping with

Sloan, but this, the absence of Ivy's name on my Facebook profile. I couldn't bring myself to switch over to single and instead opted for the comforting allure of nothingness, a refusal to answer.

I wandered around the house, unsure how I would fill not only the long day before me but the parade of empty weeks and months to follow. I went outside and took in the mail. Not e-mail, but actual, physical mail delivered by a human being in uniform! A system of communications that had been reduced to bills and the yearly birthday card from my confused grandparents. I thumbed through the stack and blinked at the final letter. A credit card statement. Oz's credit card statement. The hot rush of anxiety closed on my throat. I felt it dawning on me. An ultimatum similar to the one I'd come to in front of the garage, deciding what to do in case Oz's car was still there. This is what I knew. Oz had disappeared weeks ago. He'd taken his car. Presumably, if he was still alive, he would have to make purchases which I would find on his credit card statement. If he really was dead, there'd be nothing, the blankness of a ghost. I would have to call the police and his mother. I would have to admit that once again I had failed. And if there were purchases? If his credit card had traced his itinerary to California or Alaska or Florida, what then? I ripped open the bill. It was time for the truth.

Oz had swiped his card as recently as two days ago.

I sat down on the porch and shook my head. I often imagined how different my life would be had I somehow managed to save Keith—so guilt-free and wonderful. What each of these scenarios shared was that they all began the same way: with me shouting in joy the moment I rescued him. That's not what happened after reading Oz's statement. I just smiled, feeling weightless. He'd swiped his card in Sunbury, Buttzville, Poughkeepsie, Warrensburg, a zigzagging trail that brought him close to New York City before darting northward. Then the final six expenditures, the most recent ones. A supermarket. A gas station. A sporting goods store. All in Black Brook, New York. Black Brook, New York? Where was that exactly?

Inside, I googled the town. There it was, a glob of buildings nestled in the heart of the Adirondacks all green and pixilated on my dusty computer screen. It was so obvious that I should have guessed it right from the start. His father's cabin. The same one where we'd barricaded ourselves during the second Bush election. Of course that's where Oz had run off to. Of course that's where he'd make his final stand against late-era capitalism. He wasn't dead; he was in hiding.

The man stopped pruning outside, and for the first time since meeting with Elaine earlier that week, a feeling of peace and serenity warmed my body, almost pinking my skin. Atonement for everything I had done the night before with Sloan, for everything I had failed to do for Keith was still possible. I could drive to the cabin and save Oz. I could make things right and prove that I was a legitimate human being with feelings, not some internet avatar made flesh. Here was the second chance I'd longed for, another opportunity to reel in one of my friends from the brink. I remembered the promise I'd made to Elaine in the greenhouse, that I would go see her mother. I could do that too! I could stop off in Scranton after rescuing Oz! In one broad stroke I could attain redemption!

I dressed quickly and ran outside to my car. There, the aforementioned man in flannel was sitting in the flatbed of his truck pawing a sandwich. He waved at me in the morning sun.

"Where you off to, kid?"

"I'm going to the Adirondacks to become a more fully realized person!"

He considered this for a moment before raising his half-eaten sandwich in salute. "Uh, good luck with that."

I floored the gas and drove toward the golden blaze of the sun. I never looked back.

Four years had passed since Oz and I spent a strange two nights in the Adirondacks, but very little had changed. Here were the same highways littered with fast food stops. Here was the dirt road that seemed to stretch on forever. The only difference was that now I was alone, Oz replaced with the GPS, its *Terminator* voice barking at me with each new turn. Recalculating! Recalculating!

I arrived at the cabin shortly before sunset, my tires caked with mud, the Saturn smelling of sweat and half-devoured gas station food. I blocked in Oz's Cavalier, careful not to run over the fire pit he'd constructed nearby. I knelt alongside the remains of the fire. Tiny pieces of bone, no bigger than the teeth of a child, sparkled in the ash. I picked one up and inspected it, smooth and clean. It wasn't exactly the picturesque campsite I'd hoped for.

If Oz really was in there, he didn't give any indication. I paused outside the front door and took a deep breath, tried to calm my shuddering heart. A gust of wind swept through the campsite toward the pond down the hill. Oz. This was it.

The door creaked open like in a thousand horror films. Oz sat in an arm chair on the opposite side of the cabin reading a comic book with the last of the day's light. He put it down and glared at me. Only a few weeks had passed since his exodus from the bridges of Pittsburgh, but already Oz looked different. Mostly it was the hair. He'd shaved off his once unruly beard and even his thick hair, whittled it down to a crew cut and some stubble along his cheeks. He looked younger without it, boyish, his oversized glasses marooned on the upper half of his face. He was thin, so much thinner than I remembered, his husky body reduced to something closer to mine. Only on Oz it didn't look natural, didn't look human. The cabin smelled rank.

"You shouldn't have come. How did you even find me?"

"Your credit card statement."

He shook his head, wouldn't meet my eyes. "I'm not leaving."

I put up my hands. "All right, let's not jump the gun." I squinted at the comic. Spider-Man swung through the sky-scrapers of New York City clutching the bleeding out body of his clone Ben Reilly. "Is that one of my comics?"

"You left them here after the election."

I glanced around the cabin. It looked mostly how I remembered, but everything was covered in a layer of dust even more pronounced than our Election '04 sojourn. It was hard to believe that Oz, or anyone for that matter, had been living in this mausoleum for weeks.

"This is when I eat dinner," Oz said.

"Can I join you?"

"I only have enough for one."

"I saw a diner not too far from here. Want to go for a ride?" I figured it was the best strategy. To lure Oz away from his Thoreau-esque nightmare and into my car, down the highway, and inside a well lit diner where he could remember all the pleasures of living within the confines of society. Like gravy fries and a turkey club.

"No." He stood up and popped open a metal ice box, pull-ing out a slim cotton bag. "Fish," he explained.

"Is that sanitary?" I asked, trailing him outside.

"Yeah. You don't keep game in plastic. I bought the ice blocks in town along with some saw dust. I fish every morning."

"In that shitty little pond?"

"There's a stream two miles north. Trout. They're easy to filet."

He set the bag down to thaw in the last light. I watched

him organize the wood in the fire pit. He lay one block horizontally and leaned three others against it vertically. He retrieved a half-destroyed comic book from under a rock and ripped up the pages into shreds, stuffing them between the wood. A few seconds later—with the aide of a tiny Bic lighter—he had a small and steady flame going.

"How do you know how to do all this stuff?"

"I watched some YouTube videos on my iPhone."

Darkness swept through the camp reminding me of the long ago day when we'd huddled in my car listening to election results over the fuzzing radio. Four years later and the only sound came from the flames, crackling, the swift hiss of juices and water escaping the cooking trout wrapped in tinfoil.

"A lot's happened since you've been gone," I said. "I got fired from my job. Then me and Ivy broke up. She'd been chatting with her ex on Facebook for months. Said she didn't love me."

He kept his eyes on the trout and the fire, the flames reflected in his dust-spotted glasses. "I'm sorry," he managed.

I hadn't intended on telling him the truth about Sloan, that I'd slept with her not once, but twice, that she planned on leaving Noah and moving in with her mother. But seeing him this way—even more detached than normal and verging on a folksy insanity—made me reconsider. I was suddenly willing to do anything to shake him out of this funk, to crack his exterior and resurrect the Oz I had come to love in those heady days of Tower A.

"That's not all that happened," I said. "I never told you this, but I slept with Sloan in college. Just one time. Before you told me how you felt about her." I trailed off. "And I did it again. After me and Ivy broke up. I was really drunk. She said she was going to break up with Noah and stay with her mother awhile."

Oz crouched down low beside the fire. He grabbed the

tinfoil with his bare hands and flipped it over. He sat back down and for a long time said nothing. "That would have bothered me a long time ago," he finally said. "Before I came out here and made my transformation, gave up the petty squabbling that so often defines us. But honestly, I'm not that surprised. In a way, the two of us have been in love with her since freshman year. You actually pulled the trigger I guess."

His shoulders were slumped forward, his t-shirt spotted in brown dirt. It became clear that it wasn't the cabin that had smelled but Oz. I wanted so badly to provide him some comfort, some assurance that not everything in this world had been rigged to make him depressed.

"I think we were all in love with each other," I told him. "The three of us. Noah. Even Ivy toward the end."

"I had a feeling something like this was going to happen. The end of our little gang. The longer we stayed together, the longer we stayed in stasis. We couldn't evolve beyond the person the others saw. When I looked at you or Sloan I saw the same kids I met in Tower A seven years ago. You thought the same of me I'm sure."

"But we're still friends. Right?" I asked.

"You mean in the present tense?"

"Yes, the present tense."

Oz finally looked at me, his eyes exasperated, the way teachers get with students who refuse to listen. "Dinner's ready." He retrieved the tinfoil from the flames, and using his shirt, peeled it open. He ate with his dirty fingers. One single filet. How could that be enough? How could that Lilliputian amount of protein actually sustain him? He finished quickly and tossed the garbage in the fire, explained that he burned the skeletons as soon as he gutted them.

"So is that your daily routine?" I asked. "You read my old Spider-Man comics then burn up fish bones?"

"I don't expect you to understand this, but my new life here is extremely fulfilling. There's no pressure. I'm not expected to do anything out here. I wake up at dawn and fish, and when I get hungry I cook. That's about it. Sometimes I split firewood. Sometimes I dig up worms. Sometimes I read comics. Very rarely I need to go into town to buy supplies. Most of the time I'm free to just absorb nature and ponder life. This is what I was meant to do."

He picked up a twig and produced a Swiss army knife from his back pocket. Then he did something I'd never seen in my life outside of old cartoons and black and white movies. He started whittling. Owen Osborne III was whittling! How long had he contemplated exile, and what did it say about me that I hadn't even noticed until it was too late?

"What are you going to do in the winter?" I asked.

"Huh?" Oz looked up.

"When it gets too cold to fish? When it's too cold to live in the cabin?"

"I'll build a fireplace inside." The scrape, scrape, scrape of his pocket knife. "This is my life now, Michael."

I tried to hide my frustration and poked at a caterpillar on the ground. Oz's newfound fantasy of living off the land sounded little more than an extreme reaction to his digital frontier bullshit of the last few years. Despite his lack of hair and newfound predilection for whittling, this was still my Oz, and I still believed I could bring him back. I steeled myself. It was time to do what I'd driven across state lines for.

"So why did you leave anyway? Is this because of that bad grade?"

"I was unhappy for a long time. Even before the grade." He didn't take his eyes off the wood. "I felt like there were no more choices left in my life, like I'd been locked on a very rigid path. And I don't mean just because I went for my PhD in English which means there's only one route forward, grad school, dissertation, adjunct, tenure. I don't mean that at all." He paused here to take a sip from his canteen. He offered it to me and there was the unmistakable taste of whiskey mixed in with water. "I mean there's no choice left to be a good or kind person in this world. It's fundamentally impossible."

"I don't understand."

"Let's say I continue to live my life like I did back in Pittsburgh. I go to a department store and buy a shirt. It was probably produced by some slave child in the third world. I fill up my gas tank. Then I'm depositing money directly into the pockets of Middle Eastern dictators and contributing to global warming. Let's say I get married and buy my wife a ring. It's made from blood diamonds and my purchase sustains that gruesome industry. How about a house in the 'burbs? That's a vote to divide America across racial and class lines. Ok, move to the ghetto. Then I'm a gentrifier forcing poor people out of their homes." He laughed once, twice, quickly, like he'd discovered a joke only he understood, one that wasn't very funny at all. "It doesn't matter what you do in this world, you can't choose to be a good person. True human connection is impossible because everything we do has a negative outcome. The only rational response is to completely and utterly abstain from everything and everyone." He gestured around him. "Welcome to my conscientious objection."

"What about your iPhone? Isn't that causing a negative outcome?"

"I have eight months left on my contract."

A piece of wood cracked in half, sending a flicker of red embers into the night sky. We watched them float up and up and up before Oz gently placed another piece of wood atop the flames. I didn't know how to respond. He was so good at logic and reasoning, but everything he'd said was so nihilistic. I wanted him to come back with me. I wanted him to have some lightness about him and return to Pittsburgh and be my partner in *Contra* for Nintendo. I wanted him to be happy and ok.

"Let me ask you something," he said. "After everything

that's happened with you and Ivy and Sloan and Noah, after all the crap in your web comic about how the internet and video games have reduced us to robots, do *you* really think a genuinely good and positive human connection is still possible?"

For a long time I didn't reply, I just stared into the fire. In many ways, Oz had pinpointed the central problem I'd wrestled with my entire life, maybe since that long ago day when I first powered up my Nintendo and slipped into the neon colored world of the digital. I would have never been able to articulate it myself, but now that Oz had, the truth emerged in my chest as though it had always been there, dormant, just waiting for the right question so it could bubble up to the bright, raw surface of the world. I tried to think about all the bad things, but the good times were so much more vibrant. Laughing through *Terminator 2*. Going to Pirates games. Dinner parties that ended with us driving through snowstorms singing unembarrassed at the tops of our lungs. Making love to Ivy and feeling led into a world of endless possibility. So many nights in the Squirrel Cage talking and feeling so safe and so loved. All those moments we shared. All of us, even Keith. Didn't they accumulate? Weren't they worth something even in the face of Oz's undeniable doom? Didn't they add up into something good, an algebraic equation of life and death tipped in favor of hope?

"I'm not really sure if human connection is still possible, but I have to keep trying." I looked him in the eyes. "I used to have this friend back in high school. I never told you about him. He killed himself. I can't let that happen to someone I care about again."

Something hooted in the distance. Another block of wood cracked. Oz tore up another sheet of the comic book and sprinkled it into the fire. We watched it burn, watched the four-color faces of Peter Parker and Ben Reilly dissolve into nothing and fade into the starry sky.

"I've been rereading your Spider-Man comics," he told me. "They're not very good. They don't make sense to me. The way Peter broods about not being able to save Ben Reilly. They were like brothers and then Ben dies, but it wasn't Pete's fault. That's not on Pete." He took another sip from his canteen. "That's always been your problem. You think you either have to save someone or that someone's coming to save you. Superheroes aren't real, Michael. You can only save yourself."

"You're not coming back with me, are you?"

"I'm letting you off the hook."

I stayed there a little while longer, just enough for the fire to die down into embers, for Oz to turn a bucket of water upside down over the fire pit and plunge us into darkness. He led me to the Saturn. I opened the door and the dome light illuminated our faces.

"Your friend," Oz said as I climbed inside. "What was his name?"

I started the engine. I put the car in reverse. "His name was Keith Tedesco."

I watched Oz disappear in the rearview mirror. The dirt road was harder to navigate in the dark, and I didn't make it back to the highway for another two hours. I was leaving without Oz but there was still one thing I could do, the thing I should have done the moment he went missing in the first place. I sped toward the nearest hotel while I called Oz's mother in Maryland, the dowdy woman I remembered from move-in day, graduation, all those empty markers of adulthood. I explained the situation, Oz's bad grade, his guilt over living in an imperfect world, his self-imposed Adirondack exile. She assured me she would go after him, that she would take him home and "fix" this. I didn't believe her, but I'd done everything I possibly could. Unlike with Keith, this time there would be no regrets. Soon, I was checked in at the hotel and inside my room, my feet dangling off the bed.

I fell into a sleep so deep and so comfortable that for a brief moment the next morning I opened my eyes and thought I'd awoken to a world distant in the future: painless, effortless, beautiful.

Check out time was in ten minutes, but the teenage clerk was held up by a young married couple arguing over some detail about their son's birthday party in the hotel pool. There was no one else in line, so I wandered around the tiny lobby and filled up on complimentary coffee. A gang of four ginger-haired boys sat on a couch in front of a closed off fireplace. They wore birthday hats and too bright t-shirts decorated with dinosaurs in the vein of Jack Kirby. They were obviously brothers. What interested me about them was how they'd sequestered themselves off from the other young partygoers, how they'd taken refuge in the lobby to play some card game with drawings of multi-colored monsters. It looked incredibly complicated. They all had cell phones—the kind with miniature keyboards that slid out from palm-sized screens—and often they would halt their game and consult these devices, their thumbs dancing wildly over the keys. I remembered playing a similar card game in grade school, and with nothing better to do while waiting to check out, decided to ask them about it.

"Howdy," I said. They glanced at me before returning to their phones. "Whatcha playing there? Is that *Magic: The Gathering*? I used to play that back in the day."

More typing. Finally, one of the boys laughed and told the nearest brother that he didn't know either.

"Are you texting each other?"

The tallest one nodded. "Duh."

"But you're right next to each other."

A different boy laughed, not at what I'd said but at some

text message he'd just received. "I know, right?" he said. "We were just laughing about *Magic: The Gathering*. We don't even know what that is. This is *Naruto*. We're playing *The Chosen* expansion."

"Yeah, but why do you have phones? You're children."

No one replied. The smallest brother played a card and the oldest hooted in mock anger. "Dang!" he shouted. I repeated my question.

"Why not?" the oldest brother said. "We have e-mail and Facebook."

"You've got the internet on your phones? I don't have the internet on my phone. How old are you?"

"Eleven."

"And you're talking to your Facebook friends right now?"

"Obvi."

"But aren't your friends in the pool?"

"I'm leaving them funny YouTubes on their walls."

And so it had come to this: The Next Generation. A bunch of technophiles who refused to physically socialize even at birthday parties. At least I hadn't been exposed to the terrors of the internet until ninth grade and the onset of puberty. At least I'd enjoyed the occasional game of tag or street football back in the day. I stared at these boys and wanted to warn them. I wanted to deliver a Big, Important Speech about the necessity of valuing physical friendship over the intangible allure of technology and the internet. I wanted these boys to promise they would do better, that they wouldn't make the same mistakes I had, that they'd be better equipped to deal with the legion of challenges presented to them by a post-post-post lifestyle. I wanted to tell them that everything was going to be ok, and for them to tell me the same in return.

Don't let anyone suffer! Don't let anyone die!

The oldest boy looked at me and frowned. "You want to try it?" he asked.

"Excuse me?"

He held out his phone. "Do you have Facebook? Do you want to try it on my phone?"

The other boys finally stopped tapping and paid attention to me.

"Yes," I said. "Yes, I'd like that a lot actually. Thank you."

The phone felt slippery in my hands. The screen was too small, too cramped. Facebook didn't look right—it didn't look modern. It reminded me of those old Angelfire sites in the final days of the previous century. But I was still able to navigate using a tiny trackball and logged into Keith's account. There it was, sprung eternal on this child's machine. There he was, smiling and alive, his suicide hovering unknown in the future.

The teenage clerk tapped me on the shoulder. "Are you ready to check out, sir?"

I told him I was. I thanked the children and returned the phone, left them to their card games. They were on their own.

I crossed the state line back into Pennsylvania and fed my iPod into the mess of wires that spewed from the dashboard radio. In my head I kept circling back to the *Mega Man* series on Nintendo, how the game was non-linear, no set path, how you could choose your bosses in any order. I'd tackled Oz and now I had to press start on the pixilated image of Mrs. Tedesco in my mind. I clicked a playlist titled "2001 or THIS IS HOW THE CENTURY IS BORN" filled with all the cringe-worthy emo songs I had adored in those blossoming years of my tragic teenage youth. They were all so melancholy, so raw, so earnest. I sped up on the highway. Up and up and up. Like Keith used to do in his Prelude before he died. And in that moment I could almost feel him next to me, his still ingrained presence, the sensation of closing my eyes, screaming the words to some song loaded with cheesy meaning, Keith forcing us forward into the future.

I saw the dying lights of Scranton alongside the highway an hour before sundown. I parked across the street from Keith's childhood home and remained in the car gathering up all of my courage. It was time to eschew my Pinocchio past once and for all. It was time to do what I'd avoided since those carefree pre-9/11 days.

It was time to confess to Mrs. Tedesco.

She didn't move away after Keith suffocated in the garage. Nor did she leave when her husband of two decades suffered a massive stroke one sunny summer day mowing the lawn. I didn't know how she could stand it in there. The constant reminders. The tremors of their daily routines. In some tangible way didn't their spirits still inhabit that house? Didn't she wake up in the middle of night, reach out for her husband and feel nothing but cold, haunted mattress?

A stone path led to the front door, and the smooth surface beneath my feet comforted me. Mrs. Tedesco was not Mrs. Havisham; she hadn't allowed the exterior of her home to fall into disrepair. She still had Elaine after all. The grass was neatly trimmed, the bright, big yard free of debris. The only difference was the pool. It still hummed as loudly as I remembered, but a blue tarp now covered the water. I rubbed my thighs and rang the doorbell.

I hoped I wasn't about to catch Mrs. Tedesco during dinner. I didn't think I could stomach it if I found her sitting in front of the television eating cream of mushroom soup or whatever instant food widows eat devoid of all pleasure. The curtain behind the door swayed and Mrs. Tedesco squinted at me through a pane of glass. At first, she was expressionless, but then her lips curled into what can only be described as a kind of smile, the type you might reserve for a forgotten boss from a teenage McJob.

Mrs. Tedesco opened the door in a powder blue blouse and Capri pants. Her bushy brown hair fell to her shoulders and she looked tanner than I'd ever seen anyone's mother. What was Mrs. Tedesco doing with herself these days? Just tanning? Didn't she used to work at Bishop O'Hara's rival high school as a receptionist? Funny how kids never remember the jobs of their friends' parents.

"Michael!"

"It's me."

I hugged her. I didn't remember Mrs. Tedesco being so petite, no more than five feet, much shorter than Ivy, maybe even shorter than Sloan. I held her close and smelled the perfume of her hair. Strawberry? Yes, strawberry.

She pulled free and kept her hands tight on my shoulders. "What do I owe this visit to? You don't call. You don't write."

"I just wanted to say hello, see how you were doing. Sorry for just dropping by."

I could have mumbled through a list of apologizes for the rest of time but caught myself before I spewed a thousand mea culpas Mrs. Tedesco would only hate me for. She didn't miss a beat. "Well come on in then. I was just brewing some coffee. You want a cup?"

She stroked my forearm and took me inside. She fetched a mug from the kitchen. Here was the same lumpy couch from my youth, where Keith got stoned and drunk while we watched *Terminator 2* for the millionth time. I looked around and took stock of what little had changed. She'd kept the wooden console television that was already out of date back in high school, but had jettisoned the framed pictures above it, replacing those frozen images of her husband and son—even her living epidemiologist daughter—with a reproduction of a painting. A blue background with a red slash down the left hand side, a handful of black dots on the right. How on earth did Mrs. Tedesco end up with *this* in her house? A woman who enjoyed greeting cards and attended the same Saturday church services her entire life. Did proximity to death push people closer to aestheticism?

"Here you go, honey." Mrs. Tedesco set three mugs on the table and sat close to me. I sipped my coffee—some fruity blend I'd typically gag on—and relished this opportunity to be silent and ponder. But why the three mugs? Had Mrs. Tedesco gone insane and set one out for Keith? No. I refused to give into a Poe-like inclination for the gothic.

"I'm having company over soon," Mrs. Tedesco said.

"I'm not intruding, am I?"

She patted my arm. "Of course not. So tell me, what's new with you? Catch me up on the story of Michael Bishop."

I was already sweating. "What I really came here to talk to you about was Keith."

"Sure, love," she said. "His accident changed our lives forever."

Accident. It was as I'd feared. Mrs. Tedesco still believed that Keith's death was an accident, not a suicide I might have prevented. But before I could reveal the truth, the doorbell rang. Mrs. Tedesco hurried to answer it, a healthy bounce in her step. A man emerged who in so many ways reminded me of my father. Tall and muscular under a short-sleeved button down shirt that looked like it had been purchased in Sears. It wasn't hard to picture him in Carhartts and Wolverines, digging around under a car or hammering away at a piece of wood. His face was creased and his dark mustache was so thick, so burly, so manly that I imagined miniature orphans swinging from those locks, making their homes in the bristle like the Ewoks.

"Michael, I'd like you to meet my friend, Jim."

I stood and pumped Jim's hand. He smiled at me, and I wondered if I knew him somehow, if he was the father of some forgotten classmate from Bishop O'Hara or if all men over forty in Scranton just naturally turned out this way, rugged and strong and good. I stared at him. Was it possible that not only had Mrs. Tedesco taken a lover but that she'd somehow managed to move on from the deaths of both her husband and son?

"Michael was best friends with Keith," Mrs. Tedesco explained as we sat down—I took particular notice of how she and Jim squeezed together on the love chair.

"It's nice to learn about him from a friend's perspective, hear all those little details a mother can miss. It's the same way with Elaine. I run into one of her old friends at church and hear some story I never knew about."

Jim took a mighty sip from his steaming coffee. "Don't let me interrupt then. Go on, son."

"Well," I said, "there's something about Keith that I don't think you know about, and I feel like I kind of have to tell you."

I'd rehearsed this speech a hundred times on the drive from New York. The way I would explain Keith's coming out and my idiotic reaction and how terrible I still felt, how guilty, how I would do anything to go back in time and change things. I knew every single word, every single pause, every single gesture. But what I hadn't been ready for was this: seeing Mrs. Tedesco's face, the way she leaned in, how eager she looked. What I hadn't even considered was the possibility that Mrs. Tedesco had been able to move on. I suddenly wanted to stand up and run, to dive through the window of my car and speed all the way home to Pittsburgh. I spilled a few drops of coffee on my pants. What good would it do to tarnish the image of her son, to transform his accidental death into a preventable suicide, to make her as guilty as me? In a way, it seemed crueler to actually tell her. Mrs. Tedesco was living proof that it was ok and maybe even advisable to move on. And of course, I wasn't completely alone in knowing the truth about Keith's suicide. I *had* told Ivy Chase.

What a terrible bond to bind two people together. Maybe that's what soured our love, the virus spreading, spreading until the entire hard drive had to be scraped.

But Mrs. Tedesco and Jim were both still looking at me, and I knew I had to tell them something. "Oh, um, well, I just wanted you to know that... I guess... what I'm trying to say is that I was always the screw up while Keith was the dependable one. The guy with the master plan."

Mrs. Tedesco looked as surprised by this admission as I was. She must have remembered us as the dreamiest pair of goons in town, the type of boys who wasted weeks concocting plans for hover crafts and functioning light sabers, boys who displayed their righteous failures for the whole neighborhood to see. The Keith I referenced was not the earthly one I suddenly realized, but the unattainable Keith I had constructed on Facebook, the one who never failed, the one who was perfect and everything I could never be. And in some small way wasn't this electronic persona just as valid as the real Keith? Didn't he hold some weight in the world if he possessed the ability to give myself and Mrs. Tedesco some legitimate closure? The solution finally presented itself. What I would do. What I had come there to do. It was not enough to reimagine Keith on the internet. I had to reimagine myself as well and take Keith's crosses on as my own. I would remake my life in the crimson and gold of a brilliant failure.

"There was this one time," I began, "back in high school when I was really confused. It was the Fourth of July right before Keith's accident." My fingers trembled with the pleasure of telling stories again. I felt transported to the second floor of the Squirrel Cage with Oz and Sloan and Noah and Ivy talking bullshit deep into the night, so genuinely happy. "I'd never had a girlfriend before and I had this suspicion, just a suspicion mind you, that I might be gay."

Jim leaned forward. Mrs. Tedesco crossed her legs. The two of them were mine now, their collective joy glowing atomic. Everybody loves a good story. They're how we make sense of this flawed world.

"I drove over here with some fireworks and beer and asked Keith to go with me to Lake Scranton. He said yes of course. Because he was the type of guy who would help out any friend in a jam, you know? That's just how he was. Always put others ahead of himself. Never let a friend down."

A grandfather clock chimed upstairs. Mrs. Tedesco rubbed her moistening eyes.

"So we go up to the lake and I get drunk. Not Keith though. He was never one for beer or pot. That was me. He was always trying to get me to fly straight as an arrow. But I get drunk and set off those fireworks and I tell Keith I think I might be gay. And you know what he said to me?"

I touched the skin under my chin and brought my hand back and forth, back and forth. In this tiny moment I could resurrect Keith. I could make him live again.

"Keith says to me he doesn't care one way or another if I'm gay. If that's my way he'll stand with me to the bitter end, regardless of what the nuns or other kids at O'Hara say." My voice cracked. "Keith was such a good person and it's not fair what happened to him, what happened to all of us. I miss him every day. Sometimes I wish I'd died instead of him."

Mrs. Tedesco started sobbing. She hugged me while I sat awkwardly on the couch. We embraced for a full minute, and once Mrs. T calmed down, I thanked her for the coffee and told her I had to go, that I was sorry for intruding on her company. We made promises to keep in touch, all those well-intentioned pledges nobody ever keeps. They walked me to the front porch and waved as I drove away, but I didn't make it very far. Just a block to an empty parking lot in front of a closed supermarket. The lot overlooked the valley of downtown—the tall buildings, the green courtyard filled with all those commemorative statues—and the sun was setting over the mountains in the west divided by Route 6. Everything was bathed golden, and for once, I didn't see any irony in this. I allowed myself to just enjoy the sunset, the concrete vista. I hid my face close to the steering wheel and finally cried for everything we had lost.

I spent the night at my parents' house. I explained that I'd come to visit Mrs. Tedesco and needed a place to crash, and of course they were thrilled, made me dinner, showered me with love. When they went to bed, I booted up their old computer, that massive white monitor that took up the entire desk. I navigated to Facebook and logged into Keith's profile.

I scanned it for a few moments, tried to take in this monument to the dead I'd constructed. For so long it had been a source of shame, undeniable proof that I was strange and too far along the road to post-humanity to be saved. But now, after talking with Mrs. Tedesco firsthand, I saw his profile as something else entirely: sacrament, resurrection.

I unlocked his profile so that everyone on earth who typed in "Keith Tedesco" would find him reborn. Then I went one step further. Posing as Keith, I added Elaine and Ivy and Noah and Sloan and Oz as friends. Then I logged in as myself and posted at the top of Keith's wall. *I did this,* I typed. *It was me. I made this.* I wanted them all to know. Even Noah and Sloan who weren't even aware of the mark Keith had left on my life, who weren't even aware that a ghost boy named Keith Tedesco haunted my teenage memories. And Elaine? Surely she would think I was a monster for dredging up her past catastrophes, for parading around her suffocated brother to make myself feel more human. But I was ok with that. Her mother would probably tell Elaine about our conversation anyway, and she would recognize the way I had lied and turned everything in on itself. She would probably hate me, but that was ok too, because more than anything I just wanted them to know. All of them. Everyone. That's all I've ever really wanted. For someone to know me, understand me, to acknowledge that I exist, that my tiny little life matters.

I just want you to know how much this all means.

Election Night:
The Epilogue

The elation over Barack Obama was—might I add, predict-
ably—short lived. The highlights were over. The B Man made
his speech and left us in the Cage to gawk, to drink, to wonder.
And really, what was there to do now? For so many months,
the only thing people had talked about was the election, the
election, the election. We were raised on George W. Bush
and cynicism. What were we supposed to do now?

Ivy sipped her beer. Four hipsters in fedoras and flannel
vacated the booth on our left.

"You want to sit?" she asked.

I have no clue why Ivy didn't want to emphatically end
all chapters in her life containing that unsavory jerk Michael
Bishop. But *she* asked me to stay. I checked my watch just for
the gesture of the thing before finally nodding yes.

We sat. I ordered a pitcher. She let me pay.

"Tell me about your life, Michael. Tell me about what's happened these last six months."

At last we had come to the moment I'd longed for since her arrival, the joyous occasion when I could unleash just what exactly I'd been doing since the End of Our Relationship. I pulled my iPhone out of my back pocket and set it on the table.

"Why don't you see for yourself?" I asked.

Ivy held it close to her face and saw that I'd replaced *Michael Bishop's Wacky World of Robot Human Hybrids* with *Michael Bishop's Digital Narcissists*, a weekly tell-all about the trials and tribulations of Generation Facebook. Over the last six months I'd developed a following in the low thousands. I pimped my product all over message boards and now, twenty episodes in, had started doing interviews with some comic fan sites, the smaller ones, nothing to get too excited about as I supported myself through a pointless job at Hillman Library. But at least it was a start. Maybe by the following year I'd have sponsorship. Maybe within two years I'd see print. Maybe I could help people begin to understand themselves.

I watched Ivy read the latest comic lifted directly from our lives. The Cage rolled on around us, all boisterous noise and the distortion of some band I didn't recognize. I remembered the days when I knew every single group, every single album, every single song on the Cage's electronic jukebox. I looked around the bar at all those people. I recognized no one.

Ivy looked up. One part pride, one part shame, one part regret. An honest smile, not her usual smirk. Those eyes. Those teeth. This was Ivy Chase.

RELIGION

WHAT'S WRONG?

ARE YOU KIDDING ME? I THOUGHT YOUR DAD WAS GOING TO START SPEAKING IN TONGUES.

I DON'T SEE WHY YOU'RE MAKING SUCH A BIG DEAL.

ARE YOU KIDDING ME? YOU READ. YOU READ!

FLANNERY O'CONNOR AND LEO TOLSTOY WERE DEVOUT CHRISTIANS.

DO YOU STILL HAVE THESE SAME HANG UPS FROM HIGH SCHOOL?

NO, I JUST HAVEN'T MET AN HONEST-TO-GOODNESS BELIEVER SINCE MOVING HERE.

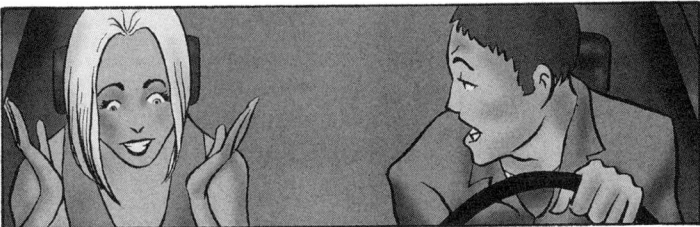

"Your comic is about us?"

"My life in general I guess."

"No irony? No hiding behind robots?"

"No." I drank my beer. "I'm trying to be more sincere, more honest about myself."

"Wow." She shook her head. "You've changed."

We looked at each other shyly then like teenagers on a first date, not scorned lovers who had tasted each other's flesh, who had almost convinced each other of the existence of love.

I heard her phone vibrating inside her purse. She took it out and tapped out some message with her dainty thumbs, and I wanted so badly to ask if it was Tommy Mendocino, if he was still in her life. I drank my Yuengling and tried not to evoke his name.

"Who's that?"

She slit her eyes at me. "Elaine. She wanted to know if I needed to be rescued from you. I tried to tell her you didn't mean any harm with that Facebook stunt with her brother, but yeah, she didn't take it very well."

I nodded. "So did you say you needed rescuing?"

"No."

"Oh. Well. Awesome," I stammered. "What about Tommy? Is he still in the picture or what? Not that I'm interested, I'm just wondering is all."

Cue the smirk. "Tommy and I are engaged. Ring's not ready yet. I'm moving back to New York next month."

I had often imagined this very moment, running into Ivy Chase again. It went a billion different ways in my head. Sometimes I was angry. Sometimes she was angry. Sometimes she wanted me back. Sometimes I rejected her. Occasionally, I even fantasized about flying a jet pack over the hypothetical New York apartment she shared with Tommy and devouring it with napalm. But in the actual moment I felt shockingly happy for her. I'd loved her, and the sad truth that she didn't feel the same way about me couldn't change that. I understood I couldn't make her happy. And although I hoped I would soon meet the saint who could put up with Michael Bishop and his antics for all eternity, it was enough for now just to know that Ivy Chase had found solace, that Ivy Chase could be happy. Didn't she deserve it? Didn't we all deserve it?

"That's great," I said.

"Thank you." She finished her beer and stood. "I think I'm going to get going. It was great seeing you though. Honestly. And I'm happy for you," she said. "Walk me to my car?"

So, just like in the Olden Days, Ivy Chase and I left the Squirrel Cage. Only now it would be for the final time.

It was colder outside than I remembered and I held my pea coat close to my chest. It had started flurrying and we hurried over to Ivy's car across the street. She opened the door and squeezed inside, but unlike our first night together, this time the Metro's engine turned flawlessly. She lowered the window and looked at me fighting shivers in the dark— the streetlight overhead had gone dead. She offered me one final half-grin before rolling up the window. Then she backed out of her parking spot and headed for the highway in the distance. Just like that she was gone, and I knew I would not see her again. She had taken leave of me. Just like Noah and Sloan and Oz and Keith, my digital ghosts, people I could now only follow on blogs and Twitter and Facebook, people who only existed for me in the megabytes and dissonance of data.

I walked back to my apartment and saw no Obama supporters along the way. They'd left, their joy deflated like the dead election balloons in the gutter. As a child, even before my mom was saddled with that terrible limp, she used to tell me to release balloons into the sky instead of popping them and throwing them away. The two of us would stand in the driveway or alongside our car if we'd just left the rare fair or circus. Then I'd let go and the balloon would float up and up and up, growing smaller and smaller and smaller until it was just a pinprick, then the sweet freedom of nonexistence. She said balloons flew all the way up to the saints and my father's father and all those wonderful people in the sky waiting for us to come home again. And wasn't that the least we could do, she asked. Wasn't it the least we could do to send those golden people a collection of balloons, tangible proof that we still honored them, tangible proof that we still loved and would always love our dead?

Acknowledgements

First, I want to thank my mom and dad. I don't know anyone who has more supportive parents and without your continued encouragement, I honestly don't know where I'd be.

Thanks to Jeff Condran and Robert Peluso for taking a chance on the novel. You won't find more gracious, intelligent, and downright fun editors anywhere on the planet. I'll put in the call for our thirty-five shots.

Thanks to Jenni Ferrari-Adler, my smart and patient agent. You helped steer the book toward its best possible incarnation, and your sage advice has been more appreciated than you know.

Thanks to Cathy Day who read so many drafts of *Last Call* and responded to so many harried e-mails and phone calls over the years. You're the one who pushed me to write this book in the first place, and you're the kind of teacher I aspire to be.

Thanks to Chuck Kinder who spent so much time getting me drunk and talking about the novel and writing in general. You told me the first draft needed more kung fu, and I hope this version satisfies you.

Thanks to Irina Reyn and Nick Coles for providing such valuable feedback on *Last Call* right from the very beginning.

Thanks to Stewart O'Nan for selecting the first chapter of the book for the Turow-Kinder award. Your kind words and guidance are always appreciated.

Thanks to Lamair Nash, my frequent collaborator, for bringing Michael's webcomics to life. You are one of the most talented artists I know, and I am forever thankful that you adopted Michael's style.

Thanks to Tom Bailey and Gary Fincke. Being part of the Writers' Institute absolutely changed my life, and I'm thankful every day for that opportunity. You taught me how to read deeper, write better, and live more fully.

Thanks to Janine Wetter for encouraging me when I needed it most. I still remember the day you singled out my writing in front of the entire class.

Thanks to Molly Lindley, Adam Schnier, Chris Lee, Katie Coyle, Dave Keaton, Amy Whipple, Jordan Mollot, Dustin Kaster, and everybody else who read versions of *Last Call* over the years. Your feedback kept me going.

Thanks to Joel Coggins for designing this very beautiful book. You've grown up before my eyes, kid.

Thanks to the many friends who shared a drink with me in the Squirrel Cage.

And a very special thanks to Kanye West, the greatest rapper ever.